SIREN'S SILENCE

SIREN'S
SILENCE

A NOVEL BY

RICHARD QUAN

Q VISION PRESS & MULTIMEDIA
Roswell, Georgia

Q VISION PRESS & MULTIMEDIA
300 Colonial Parkway, Suite 100
Roswell, GA 30076

A Richard Quan First Edition, May 2006

Copyright © 2006 by Richard Quan

Publisher's Cataloging-in-Publication
(Provided by Quality Books, Inc.)

Quan, Richard.
   Siren's silence : a novel / by Richard Quan.
   p. cm.
   LCCN 2006900425
   ISBN-13: 978-0-9777409-0-1
   ISBN-10: 0-9777409-0-0

   1. Man-woman relationships—United States—Fiction.
2. September 11 Terrorist Attacks, 2001—Influence—
Fiction. 3. Romantic suspense fiction. 4. Love stories, American.
I. Title.

PS3617.U35S57 2006   813'.6
                         QBI06-600057

Printed on acid-free paper.
Printed in the United States of America

Book Design by Arrow Graphics, Inc.
Cover Photo by Alexei Afonin
Cover Painting by Trong

TABLE OF CONTENTS

DEDICATION

A DECADE BACK, a wonderful family in Stillwater, Minnesota, opened up its door to a young college student from down South for his summer door-to-door sales adventure. Jerry, I have not forgotten about your John Wayne collections. Brett, thanks for fixing up my Honda two-door hatchback after I backed it into a metal pole in St. Joseph Township. Demo, your barks kept me up on stormy nights. Julie, I hope you will forgive me for driving a wheelbarrow into your living room wall while unloading a truck full of books out of your house. To the tens of thousands of urbanites, suburbanites, and farmers in Minnesota and Wisconsin, thanks for inviting me into your home or chasing me out of your barn. Because of you, there is a story to tell.

EVERYTHING HAS ITS TIME

For everything there is a season, and a time for every matter
under heaven:

A time to be born, and a time to die;

A time to plant, and a time to pluck up what is planted;

A time to kill and a time to heal;

A time to break down, and a time to build up;

A time to weep, and a time to laugh;

A time to mourn, and a time to dance;

A time to cast away stones, and a time to gather stones together;

A time to embrace, and a time to refrain from embracing;

A time to get, and a time to lose;

A time to keep, and a time to cast away;

A time to rend, and a time to sew;

A time to keep silence, and a time to speak;

A time to love, and a time to hate;

A time of war, and a time of peace.

Ecclesiastes 3:1-8

Part I

A TIME OF WAR

Manhattan 2003

Chapter I

CITY OF LIGHT

I T IS RAINING. It is raining hard. Sometimes I like the rain, and sometimes I don't. It is late summer. The wind is blowing and I am alone. What is happening with the weather is happening within me. Nature, too, can cry. Our moods are the same. Its tears pour over the roofs of the endless skyscrapers that tower over this great city. They grate and blend with the cars honking, the trucks squeaking, and the wheels splashing against the wet asphalt. In the backdrop of things, I can hear myself think. Feet on my desk, arms crossed, and eyes level against the windowpane, I am intensely thinking. My cell phone rings. Green digits light up the liquid crystal screen. That is odd. Who can it be? It is a number I do not recognize.

"Hello?" I greet.

Silence.

"Hello?" I repeat.

Light breathing stalks the rain.

"Who's this?"

There is still no answer. It must be one of those crazy women that I've met in the bar. They have frequently approached me, mostly middle-aged women looking for a rich young man to fulfill their needs. Word gets around fast when you are one of the most eligible bachelors in town. There is no escape. The media people are partly accountable for my unwanted fame. Those reporters and journalists hounded me. They smeared my face on the front page of every major newspaper in town. I even had the privilege of seeing myself on TV. I know everyone needs to make a living, but I wish they would just leave me alone. Give it a rest and let me breathe, for Christ's sake.

The work I do and the people I represent got me into this mess in the first place. I am a private person and prefer to be left alone. I want to walk into a restaurant without people eyeing me, and I wish to enter a bar without being constantly pursued by strange women. With all the media coverage, I have to be careful. News articles put crazy thoughts into people's heads. Everyone wants to be famous. Everyone wants to be rich. Everyone wants a piece of the action. A lot of gold diggers are out there. Everything is a game, a chase, and a race to get something or someone. Everyone puts on a good show, but behind the multi-layered façade, the artificial attentiveness, and the materialistic displays of Rolex watches and thousand-dollar suits lies the true motive. The bottom line is women want to get a hold of men's wallets, and men want to get inside women's pants. That is how things work around here. Whether I accept it or not, that is how things operate in the city of New York. It is all about power, money, and lust. These three great sins run the city that never sleeps. They whip in the blender of life and fill the cocktails that its occupants drink. Big or small, each wants something from the other. The small fish wants a piece of the big fish, and the big fish wants a piece of the bigger fish. Whatever the size may be, one would have to be crazy and naïve to think that true love floats with a free spirit and Bloody Mary. Love and alcohol simply do not mix. The end result is a temporary illusion of love, sex, and a morning-after pill.

Sometimes I wonder if I have chosen the right profession. I even wonder if I have made the right choice by moving here. I do not know how much longer I can put up with all of New York's craziness, the media frenzies, the courtroom brawls, the restless crowds, the noise, the crime, the terrorist threats, and the endless piles of paperwork. Everything is getting to me. Not even the delicate hands of my personal masseuse can remove the tension in my neck. I am like a duck, appearing calm and in control, but under the unruffled surface, I am paddling. I am paddling nonstop.

"Whoever you are, this is not funny!" I explode in annoyance.

"Hi," a sexy voice says.

My stomach churns and goose bumps crawl along my skin. It must be some sort of joke. The Voice, whoever it belongs to, sounds identical to a voice from my past. It can be no one else's but hers. I know it is hers. It has to be hers. It holds that distinct tone, not too loud and not too soft but a perfect pitch of neutrality that emerges from the threshold of an audible whisper. An element of rare calm characterizes that voice. How can that be? It is impossible. I pinch myself. Ouch. I am awake.

Outside, a hooded sky hangs low. Beneath the stirring clouds, the black birds fly. With wet wings, they fly until the dark fuzzy haze swallows them whole.

Behind the glass door my secretary is typing away. I see her hands moving, but I hear no sound. My gaze returns to a painting on the wall. She looks real. She, the face I believe is behind the voice in the phone, looks so real that I can reach out and touch her. She is not real, though. She cannot be real. She is only a reflection of reality that once existed. She is nothing more than dried paint on a piece of canvas. On that canvas, she stands immortal in a black satin dress. Her back is reflected in a body-length mirror. Her eyes beam from the shade of her hat, and her lips burn with the fury of a bloody sun.

"Siren, is that you?" I ask.

"No, but I have news," the Voice says.

Part II

A TIME OF PEACE

Durham 1991-92

Chapter 2

ON THE NATURE OF THINGS

M Y NAME IS VICTOR FRANTISKA. You can call me Victor. There are four things you need to know about me. One, I am a Leo. Two, I am highly educated. Three, I am filthy rich. Four, I am stunningly handsome, as I have been told repeatedly by the women in my life. All of that does not matter though. What really matters is what I am about to tell you. The truth is, everything begins with a seed, a single spark, a germination of provocative thought, an unfolding of the imagination, and a twist of fate. All things begin with what we humans call love, and from love the petals of life unfold. Have you ever fallen in love with someone? Have you ever fallen so madly in love with someone that your heart ached, your mind blurred, and your knees weakened? Then, in the blink of an eye, the time it took for the second hand of a clock to reach the next tick, did something happen, something terrible? Just like that, your world turns upside down, and your life changes forever.

It is painful, isn't it? It is painful to even think about it, about the strange phenomenon we call love. Simple as it might appear, this four-letter word, a concept conjured up by man to describe the innate nature of an abstract feeling, can be quite deceiving. It is complex in nature. It is more perplexing than all the universe's mysteries combined. Why is it so complex? Because it is the way things are. That is how the universe operates. It is nothing and it is everything. It is you. It is her. It is the thing that she does. It is her smile, her smell, and her touch. It is her actions and reactions. It is everything you can imagine and cannot begin to imagine. Pertinent, potent, and deceptive, this concept, this seed, this spark, this chill, and this butterfly in the gut has mystified and ratified man's existence since the beginning of time. Some people write poems. Others write books. The rest of us just let our life pass us by, thinking, wondering, and asking the "what if" question.

An old man once told me that the inimitable symphony that moved him to tears and ecstasy was the sound of an approaching love. When love ceased to exist, the embodiment of his mortal being also ceased to exist. His life was nothing more than a series of loves emerging from the tranquilities of an oasis in the desert. Through these loves he could hear the echoes of his youth crying out like the longing of a faithful Muslim unable to make a pilgrimage to the holy city of Mecca. Along with these cries come the nobility, poetry, grandeur, and tragedy of life. For as long as he could remember, the old man's life had been punctuated by one love after another. It did not matter where he went, in every small town or big city, and on every mile of pine bluff or pastureland, a love was always there. Each one sat patiently like a wise old woman hovering in the air on a magic carpet, waiting and reminding him that he was alive and that he better be prepared for what lay ahead. Whenever a feeling of peace brushed fleetingly across his conscience, the way a cool shiver ran through his forehead when he was sick, scared or angry, he knew another love was on its way. The older he grew, the stronger each love became. In his attempt to escape each love, he ran across land so flat that he felt he would run off the edge of the earth, had he kept going, but surely enough, another love sat waiting in the distance.

"I guess love is not so bad," the old man said. "After all, what is life without love? It would be dull and bleak." Just like an old wooden bench awaiting a pious worshiper to warm its surface on a Sunday morning, love awaited him. The gravity of love kept him tight to the earth and warmed his soul. She stood guard at all doors of life like the half-dog statues of the tomb of Qin. As he approached her in his battle armor and prepared to repel love from his life, love made an appraising gaze at him to display her military might. She immobilized his grim-faced minions with a thousand shooting arrows. Like a skillful archer on a horse-drawn chariot, she charged at him. While he remained aloof, pondering what to do next, a forest of spears hurtled closer to the center of his heart. Driven by an urgent sense of proliferating emergencies, the saffron-clad infantrymen in him reawakened, and he drove into battle. "Life is nothing but a series of loves," the old man said, "a thousand loves charging up a thousand rivers at a thousand times. When we look at each love individually, all we see is chaos and wild turbulence. When we look at the thousand loves as one, we see greater chaos and larger turbulence. When we step back and look at these thousand loves from a distance, though, we see a recognizable pattern emerging from a sea of chaos; the pattern of the human experience."

Chapter 3

FALERNIAN'S EFFECT

I TOO ONCE HAD A LOVE. Siren Myskina was her name and *Die Pharisaer und Zollner* was her music. Siren and I met on a drizzly Sunday morning, a quiet morning during our freshman year at Duke. Trees green and air cool, it was a morning to be remembered.

Unlike most students who slept until noon, I was making my way up the marble stairways of the Union Building. It was my weekly ritual to be up before anyone else and be the first in the East Campus food court for my bowl of hot oatmeal and a slice of crispy bacon. A few steps behind, a girl slipped and fell. I heard a cry and turned around. Our gaze met. Immediately I knew she was the one. In that second of eternal bliss, I felt her magnetic attraction pulling me in. It was a connection that I had never experienced before.

Momentarily trapped in an inferno of unfolding passion and unknown danger, my heart stopped. I froze. Raven-maned and voluptuous, with a majestically sullen face, the girl brought out the obsession in me. Perhaps I was drawn to her eerie disconnection. She appeared chilly and difficult to reach. Taken in by her own distance, she looked misplaced and bewildered by the purpose of her existence in this world. Perhaps she understood it too well and was frightened by what she knew. In her emerald green eyes I saw solitude and undisclosed suffering. Mind blurred and logic lost, I was unable to determine with certainty whether the girl before me was real or a figment of my imagination. In another second, the ticking on my watch resumed and the clouds in my mind stirred clear.

"Are you all right?" I asked.

"I'm fine, thank you," she replied, briskly getting back up onto her feet and escaping into the cafeteria.

Sucker punched by fear, I let her go without a chase. I regretted my inaction. She was on my mind every waking hour after that encounter. I wondered about that mysterious green-eyed girl I had failed to pursue.

She could not be a freshman, I presumed, because she was not in the freshman yearbook. Maybe she was one of those on the waitlist who got bumped up a spot. Or perhaps she was just a visitor, or an exchange student. I wondered. I thought about the girl I briefly met and barely knew. I thought about her for days. Images of her filled my mind. They saturated my blood, flooded my veins, and excited my nerves. I became distraught by the fact that I

was infatuated with a stranger. My compulsion was coun-
terproductive to my mental health, social life, and school-
work. She was the morphine in me that never flushed out
of my system. Bundled in a web of emotion—excitement,
fear, and confusion—I debated what I should do.

"Why? Why me?" I asked myself. A part of me was glad
that I ran into her, but another part of me jeered at the
very thought of a potential relationship that could arise
out of such an abrupt meeting. For goodness sake, I was
seventeen. I was a green apple and a wannabe man. I was
not ready to be sliced by the double-edged sword of love.

To distract myself, I spent hours by the Sarah P. Duke
Gardens pond tossing breadcrumbs into the water and
watching the ducks and fish fight over them. Before long,
my distraught mind wandered back to the dark-haired girl
fate had brought to me. I pictured us on a palm-studded
beach sunbathing under a sun-dappled sky and imagined
how beautiful she would look in a two-piece bikini facing
the blue sea. I envisioned us sharing a straw hut by the
water and dreamed of waking up next to her at the break
of dawn. I even fancied layering her naked body with
white paints. "This is my beauteous creation," I would
boast to the world. "This is my angel."

She became the foundation of my existence. She
became more important to me than philosophy, science,
politics, and art. She was the ultimate illusion I had the
honor of creating for myself. My desire and passion for
her stirred the quiet cave in the deep woods of my heart
where emotions hide.

On a fateful Sunday morning, she and I met again. It was a breezy morning with the sun peeking above the horizon. The temperature was steadily climbing. Instead of cuddling in bed listening to NPR, I took a quick shower, slipped on my button-down oxford slacks, and rushed to church. I was not a church-going type. It was not within my blood to be a believer of anything other than man and the imagination of man. My father was an atheist, my mother was an atheist, and I was also an atheist. If a preacher had approached me in the street, I probably would stop whatever I was doing and run as fast as I could. I would rather jump into a raging river and be food for the fishes than have to listen to another word about God. God to me was not black or white. I did not care if God was purple, had four legs, and walked like a cow. God was a concept conjured up by man. I had agreed to attend one Sunday service to stop my roommate's pestering. I did it for Christ's sake and for my sanity.

"There's no harm in giving yourself a chance," Keith had suggested. "Sometimes a man needs to believe in something greater than himself. You have nothing to lose but a couple hours of sleep."

Based on Keith's words I decided to give God a chance. I paced to the Duke Chapel, a gargantuan edifice that towered into the sky. At the chapel door I straightened my tie and made myself known.

"Good morning!" a powerful voice thundered.

I thought the minister was addressing me, but it could not have been me, an insignificant freshman who had never set foot in the chapel before.

"For those of you who are in town for the first time, we welcome you," the minister continued. "Sunday is a day of renewal and spiritual cleansing. Sin and sorrow are purified with hope and joy."

I looked to the left and to the right to scout for a seat. My glance landed on an old man. He sat alone on a pew far from the altar. In the back aisle he held a King James Bible and hung onto the minister's every word. His thick horn-rimmed glasses and his tousled white hair projected a prophetic air. I had seen the man before. He was the man with a golden cane, the man I had encountered in the West Campus Quad near the side entrance of the Perkins Library. It was a fine day when we met. Fragile like an old house battered by the sun and rain, he edged my way and joined me on the bench where I sat. When seated he leveled his spectacles and talked to a squirrel nearby.

"What is going on inside that little head of yours, small fellow?" the old man asked. "You think I'm God, do you? Well, don't get your hopes up."

The squirrel, standing upright on its two hind legs with a nut in its mouth, twitched its whiskers and zipped out of sight. With the squirrel gone, the old man turned his attention back to me. "I always wonder what it must be like to be a squirrel," he said. "I wonder what it is like to be six inches long and see things upside down from the side of a tree trunk. It must be nice to run around all day gathering nuts and not have a worry in the world. In its eyes I see freedom from the pain, the sorrow, and the illusions of happiness that man has to endure."

With the old man's past words echoing in the back of my mind, I ventured a step farther into the chapel hall. I looked two rows ahead and stopped at a brilliant glow that emanated from a woman's foot protruding into the aisle. Sitting shoulders still and legs crossed, the object of my dreams remained unaware of my approach. The filtered light from the stained glass windows lit her hair and defined the curve of her neck. I walked closer and realized that it was she, the green-eyed girl I envisioned to be my future wife and the mother of my unborn child. The glow that had drawn me to her was a spark of light reflecting off her ankle bracelet.

"Is this seat taken?" I politely asked.

Surprised, she turned, and looked over her shoulder. "No," she replied. She brushed aside her purse to clear the way.

In that brief moment, the tragic world bleached clean. My fear and loneliness disappeared. I sat down and listened not to the minister's words but to the train of thoughts that inundated my mind about the woman next to me. Before long, an hour passed. The service came to an end. "Eternal God," the minister prayed with his head lowered, "in whom we live and move, cleanse us from our sins and deliver us from proud thoughts and vain desires so that we may humbly draw near thee. We confess our faults, confide in thy grace, and find in thee our refuge and our strength. Through Jesus Christ our Lord, Amen." The minister reopened his eyes and addressed the congregation from behind his pulpit stand. "Our last song will be from page sixteen of your hymnal. Everyone, please join me in singing 'Ye Holy Angels Bright.'"

Once I was outside, the scuffling wind toyed with the maple leaves. Orange clouds slugged the sky. Determined not to let the woman out of my sight this time, I stayed a foot behind her. "She's playing hard to get," I convinced myself. I did not want to scare her off by moving too fast, but instinct told me, "You have to act now and you must act fast. A beautiful girl like her only comes around once." The fear of rejection held me back, though. My nerves tightened and my heart pounded. Mental distress and indecision reemerged. I knew I would lie awake many nights to come, regretting my inaction if I were to let her go without a chase. "Calm down, you fool," the devil in me sneered. "She's only a girl." I pictured myself practicing Tai Chi. Breathing slowly, I lowered my heartbeat and regained control.

"What's your name?" I uttered, trying to keep up with her pace.

"Siren," she responded.

"I'm Victor."

"Nice to meet you," Siren said, her eyes sparkling.

"Would you like to join me for brunch in the Blue and White Room?" I asked.

"I would if I could, but I can't." Off she went again, fleeing mirthfully away.

Chapter 4

KATERINA'S SOLSTICE

THERE WAS SOMETHING ABOUT SIREN that I could not lay my finger on. She appeared detached, distant, and socially ill at ease. A melancholic mask often covered her face. Perhaps the world had been harsh to her during her vulnerable years. I caught her sitting alone one morning on the stairway of Lilly Library watching the early risers stroll by. When she saw me approaching, she quickly looked the other way. I kept walking.

In a quaint sense, Siren's enigmatic personality magnetized me. "Get over her," I told myself. "There are plenty of girls out there who would love to go out with you." The ploy failed, as usual, and the thought of Siren crept back into my mind. I was determined to find out what was locked inside her head, so I followed her around. Somehow and somewhere in our cat-and-mouse courtship dance, I found myself lost in her world. To prevent myself from raising false hopes, I attempted to remain ambivalent, but it was impossible. The odds were skewed in her favor. Her elusiveness only increased my drive to win her over. I kept my distance to amuse her and gave her enough clues to let her know that I was still in the hunt. Whatever I did, though, I could not let her go.

Unlike most girls at the university, Siren did not have many friends. Her life revolved around school, work, and whatever she did in her spare time. Some nights, I followed her to the Hideaway and watched the guys I knew hit on her. Other nights I watched her drift home on some stranger's arm. Her erratic mood swings and odd behavior reminded me of a pair of car dice a girl had given me. They spun with no sense of direction or predictability. The world was Siren's playground, and men like me were her pawns.

I contemplated relinquishing my pursuit of Siren on several occasions, but our unanticipated frequent encounters kept the chase alive. The more we met, the less guarded she became. Finally, one stormy day, I made a breakthrough.

In the Triangle Area the temperature plummeted, the wind picked up speed, and the trees and telephone lines swirled in disarray. With the lousy weather at hand, there was nothing else to do but sit tight and watch the news on my fuzzy black and white TV. An Old Spice commercial came on, and a thud sounded. "Who is it?" I asked, springing to my feet. There was no answer. I dashed to the door. It was Siren, holding a green umbrella covered with rainwater. Her eyes stayed fixed on me. Whatever brought her over, I was too surprised to ask. The last time that we bumped into each other was inside the university pub on a Saturday night when I was out drinking with Keith and the boys.

"Hi," Siren broke out. She placed her umbrella on the doormat, removed her shoes and padded barefoot inside. Her gaze coasted around my room. Her vision appeared to go from the two feather pillows on my bed to the walk-in-closet at her immediate left. It was a closet big enough to hold the junk of two unruly freshmen. In fact, it was large enough to hold a twin-size bed. Inside contained Keith's football jerseys, my pair of old running sneakers, soccer shorts, and a closet full of dirty socks. "Nice place," she said.

"Thanks."

"Where's your roommate?"

"He left town last night. He has a wedding to attend."

"Is that his?" Siren pointed to a poster of a NFL player getting ready to make a pass.

"It's ours. Keith and I are sports fanatics. Occasionally we bet on teams. Football, baseball, ice hockey, you name it, we bet. We bet against each other, and against the boys down the hall."

"Aren't you two too young to be gambling?"

"Come on, everyone does it. Besides, we're pretty good at it. Keith and I believe that there's one thing in life that separates the winner from the loser."

"What's that?"

"The winner applies his ability to win, and the loser hopes his luck will enable him to win. If you think about it, all events can be predicted, and all problems can be solved, if you only use your head."

"You sound pretty sure of yourselves."

"We're confident enough to win. And winning is everything."

"Tell me more about this roommate of yours. Where's he from? What's his family like?"

"Keith was born and raised in Jackson, Mississippi, and his family is loaded." Mr. Bank, his father, was a Wall Street investment banker. His grandfather, founder and former CEO of a Fortune 500 company, had billions invested in the oil-drilling business that spanned from Sumatra Java of Indonesia to the Interior Rift of Antarctica. His great-grandfather used to run a large tobacco plantation prior to the Civil War.

Siren pointed to a framed photo on Keith's desk of a young woman with a child in a Mercedes. "Who's this woman?"

"That's Keith's mother, Isabelle, in her prettier days. She's quite a woman."

"What do you mean?"

"Before her marriage to Keith's father, she was dirt poor. She taught high school in Chapel Hill. There was no way she could have afforded her current lavish lifestyle back then. Do you know what she did a day after Mr. Bank proposed to her?

"What?"

"She quit her job and went on a shopping spree."

"I would, too, if I were married to a rich man," Siren joked.

"After she got married, she even made the maids do all the cooking and cleaning." Keith said that Isabelle refused to lift a finger around the house if she didn't have to. Despite her poor upbringing, she carried an heir of aristocracy. She acted nice, courteous, and ladylike all the time and never showed her true emotion. Her manner was superficial and sometimes distrustful.

"Is that cute little boy next to her in the car Keith?"

"No, that's his older brother. He's at Harvard. We met once during freshmen orientation and a few other times during his visits here on weekends."

"Is he anything like Keith?"

"Why? Do you want to hook up with a Harvard man?"

"Can't a woman ask a question without being suspected of having sexual interest in a man? And for the record, I got into Harvard."

"Okay, you made your point. If you must know, Keith's brother is about my height and has Keith's build. He gets as much thrills following the NASDAQ as watching the Daytona 500. Investment is his scheme, and car racing is his dream. On his nineteenth birthday, he took Keith and me out for a spin in his brand new Porsche 911. Do you know what we did? We took turns cutting donuts in the university parking lot. You should have seen the smoke from the tires. And the smell of burning rubber; it was orgasmic."

"You guys are crazy."

Siren strolled past me. A beam of light from a rift of the closet door struck her. She stopped in front of a full-length mirror and glanced in. Considering the many things I knew about people, I had no clue what to make of the person standing before me under my roof. She walked in and out of my life at her own whim. She bemused me with her odd behavior. She had me in the palm of her hand, and all I could do was stand, watch, and prepare to be amazed. She joined me at the edge of my bed and placed her hand on my lap.

Heart palpitating, I scrambled for words. "Would you like a drink?" I asked.

"Sure, what do you have?" Siren inquired.

I bent over and pulled a roll of blanket from beneath the bed. Wrapped inside was a bottle of Chardonnay. "Keith's brother brought this on his way down from Boston," I said, showing the champagne bottle to Siren. "It's straight from Corey Creek Vineyard, a thirty-acre property in Southold just two miles east of another winery on the North Fork of Long Island."

"I was there when I was a child," Siren said. "It's a charming place."

I popped the cork and poured Siren a glass. We toasted. She gulped it down. I poured her a second. Again, she quickly took it in. I poured her a third. It did not take long for the alcohol to take control. Soon enough, Siren was reclining on my bed giggling mischievously. I stroked her hair, kissed her hands, and touched her lips. Although partially subdued, Siren remained on guard. "Look out," her eyes warned. "Don't be a fool."

I knew she was one of a kind, a dangerous kind, that was bad for my health and terrible for my heart, but I proceeded anyway. I proceeded because I was curious and wanted to see how far I could go. Besides, it was too late. I allowed the unthinkable to occur. I allowed her to enter my shielded fortress. I permitted her to get too close, knowing well ahead that the trenches I had dug were too shallow to dodge potential blows.

"To conquer one's adversary, one must first know where she hides, what she eats, when she sleeps, and how she thinks," my father once told me. I knew none of the above and yet I proceeded, anyway. I was a strategist with no plan, a general with no soldier, and a soldier with no gun. I dared to venture onto a field covered with landmines. "It's green," I reasoned, "therefore it's safe." I placed myself at the mercy of my enemy.

Siren's incredible scent increased my pulse with infectious calypso. If I had died that moment I would have died satisfied. My initial instinct was to stay calm and treat her with respect, but desire weakened reason, and passion overwhelmed logic. The temptation before me shattered any hopes of self-control. Her two organic possessions— two objects completely within my reach—were magnificent. They complemented the sun, the moon, and the earth. Their enticing eclipses spread darkness in my mind before the return of neural clarity. Clearly, those objects were the heavenly constellations that emitted synergies of influence over man. Objects of redemptive tenderness, they awakened a climatic act of senseless viciousness in me. They were objects of the ultimate lure. Flowingly torturous and brilliantly composed, the timely immanence of those majestic objects stirred my appetite for something more than food. The inevitable occurred. I reached forward and grabbed her inviting breasts.

"What the hell do you think you're doing?" Siren snarled, bolting to her feet.

In a desperate attempt to redeem myself, I tried to explain. It was too late.

Siren yanked away and sped out of my room. The door slam sent a cold chill down my spine. Dumbfounded, I once more found myself alone. "Idiot!" I roared at myself. "Stupid! Stupid! Stupid!" I finally calmed down and was left pondering about my unannounced visitor and how I scared her away.

Chapter 5

PNEUMA

I T TOOK MORE THAN MY regular charm to win Siren back. Learning her likes and dislikes, I asked her out to a cozy little seafood place at Franklin Street in Chapel Hill. "They have the best crab in town," I said, "All fresh from the waters of South Carolina. I promise you'll love this place."

I was right. The friendly faces, oldies music from the jukebox, and tantalizing aroma put her at ease. I had made a reservation for a table for two. It was a small table with two crane-shaped napkins and two fine china plates. We shared a candlelit dinner of martinis, grilled corn, fried shrimp, giant crab claws, and hush puppies. As we ate, I told Siren my famous crab story. "Crabs love chicken," I began. "They love raw chicken."

The Orion Nebula in Siren's eyes shone. It blazed across the table like a furious firestorm giving birth to new stars. I had never seen her so attentive; neither had I expected that my trivial utterance of such an insignificant fact would have so much effect on her. It reawakened a disinterested mind that seemed at times a million light years away. A city girl most of her life, Siren knew little about crabs. She had no idea that crabs, creatures that spent half of their life in the water, preferred chicken to fish. All she knew was that crabs tasted good. As long as she found my crab story fascinating, I was more than happy to enlighten her with more details of crabs' carnivorous habits, crab enticement, and crab catching. Her annoying fork fiddling stopped. The wandering eyes ceased moving. Her attention was mine.

"The trick to catching crabs is to bait them with chicken thighs," I continued. "Get the best ones money can buy. Crabs, like humans, also prefer fresh things. They're pretty damn smart for a creature with two eyes and no head."

"What do you do with the chicken thighs?" Siren asked.

"You cut them in chunks and fix a piece to a fishhook with a string attached. Be sure to keep an eye on your finger. I'm sure those crabs would enjoy a piece of you, too."

"And after the chicken is firmly in place?"

"You put it in a round-mouth fish net with a long handle and cautiously lower the bait into the water. Whatever you do, keep a steady hand on the handle while you level the net to the marshland bed. Crabs, like humans, panic when stirred."

"Then what?"

"You sit and wait."

"How long?"

"A minute, two minutes, five minutes, or even an hour."

"What if they don't come out?"

"Believe me, they'll come out. They'll crawl out of their holes in all shapes and sizes. They all want a piece of the juicy chicken thigh. When they start gnawing, you whack those suckers with a broomstick."

Siren laughed. I had never seen her laugh before. It felt good to be able to make her laugh.

After dinner I drove Siren to Jordan Lake. While I drove, she sat speechless on the passenger side looking out the window. The wind blew. Her hair fluttered. A mysterious arc of light swept across the dark sky. There was not much to see, but she looked anyway. With her telescopic eyes, she studied the stars and the shady black trees that lined the road. We passed over a bridge that overlooked the lake. I pulled the car over at the opposite end, and we got out and walked to the edge of the lake. The wind blew, chopped, and whipped. The water rose with dragon scales. The leaves rattled, and the crickets chirped. Our footsteps stirred the birds in the spruces, the birches, and the pines. They flocked across the lake and disappeared into the dark. It was a perfect night to be out on a date. The silvery moon idly unmasked its face behind hazy clouds. In the distant galaxy, cosmic objects collided, stars were born and died, and the chaos of life unfolded.

We sat under the great heaven listening, looking, and wondering. Head on my shoulder, Siren remained mesmerized by the beauty and wonder of the universe. It showed in her lost stare. She gazed upward with the same awe that our earliest kind must have felt, primordial and weak. The vast night sky and its trillion shining stars must have reminded her of the power and grandeur of the universe. By comparison she was puny, a speckle of dust in the sky whose mere existence was unknown of purpose and goal. A stranger would not have known that deep inside, a little girl was crying. I placed my arm around her waist and drew her near.

"The universe is beautiful, isn't it?" Siren whispered.

"Yes, it is." I picked a disc-shaped pebble and spun it across the lake. It skipped three times and sank. I picked up another and spun it out again. It skipped twice and cut into the inky water.

"There's the constellation Pegasus," Siren said, pointing to the farthest edge of outer space.

"Where are Pegasus's wings?" I asked.

"They're there. You just have to look harder."

"What about that misty band of light that arches across the sky?"

"It's part of the Milky Way. If you look closer, you'll see star clusters, dark blotches, hazy glowing patches, and bright clouds. Legends say that the Milky Way is the road to heaven." Siren took great pride in her stargazing. She told me the universe and its endless mystery had fascinated her since she was a child. At the tender age of nine, she received her first telescope. She has held onto it ever since. "An eighth Century Tang Poet once wrote," Siren said, "By studying the organic patterns of heaven and earth a fool can become a sage. By watching the times and seasons of natural phenomena, we can become true philosophers."

I pondered Siren's words and reflected on a distant summer night when I was a child. It was a clear night with the stars burning just as bright. That was the night when my father took me out on a boat, a small fishing boat. He rowed across a mile-wide river filled with schools of fresh water fish that swam beneath the belly of the vessel. Their silhouettes glided by like red blood cells moving in veins. In an attempt to refine my hunting skill, I dived from the bow into the shoulder-deep water and caught a fish with both hands. It slid away. I climbed back onto the boat and tried again. Again the fish escaped. When I finally snatched one by the tail, I held the fish high and watched it gasp for air. It twisted and spun. It shuttered and struggled to break free. When it suffered enough, I released my grip and watched the fish dive headfirst into the ever-flowing current. Not bad for a fish, I thought. It scored a perfect ten. With the creature released I followed its peers across the silky riverbed. I walked up sand dunes that peaked here and there. On the dune I pretended to be a tree. I stretched both hands wide for the world to see. I was free, free to breathe the sweeping wind and free to do with time as I pleased. When I grew tired of being a tree, I returned to the water to join the fish. I pretended to be the king of all the fish and swam among them without a gill or a fin. When I got tired of being a fish, I returned to being the little man that I was. Hair wet and body soaked, I emerged from the crystal-clear water. I held my hand high and let my father tug me back into the boat. I sat and watched my father row, left and right. While he rowed, he taught me a song. I shared that song with Siren, and she sang along.

That autumn night, I learned a little more about the mysterious woman I adored. I learned that she liked her coffee black in the morning and that she liked to climb high mountains and study stars in the twilight. Those were the three elements of certainty about Siren. Everything else was up for grabs. We had time, though. The year was fresh. We had much to learn about each other and about the world around us, and there was no better way to learn about each other than to enjoy basketball games together.

Chapter 6

KRZYZEWSKIVILLE'S
WILDSTROM

A S NEW MATRICULATES, Siren and I wanted to know what it was like to be a true Blue Devils fan, and so we packed our bags, dirtied our sneakers, and ventured out to join my friends in Krzyzewskiville, a small village of tents stationed outside Cameron Indoor Stadium. Nothing in the freshmen orientation package prepared us for what we were about to face. For weeks at a time, sometimes in the rain and sometimes in the snow, we faced Mother Nature's wrath. We risked our health and we risked our grades for another highly sought after possession, an opportunity to be seated in the front row of one of the country's most famous indoor stadiums.

Even if we had to study with flashlights and sleep in the sub-zero weather under the poorly put together tent, we stuck together and stayed tough. No leaking rain or winter frost could deter our ultimate goal, to get our hands on those prized tickets so that we could watch our team play. A passerby might question the logic of our action and the sanity of our reasoning, but to Siren and me and the rest of the Cameron Krazies, such an act reflected an impeccable display of loyalty of a true Blue Devils fan. In the spirit of the school and in the spirit of tradition we made our sacrifice and remained true to our cause. We worked hard. We studied hard. We played hard. That was all it was about. Nothing more. Nothing less.

Not all games were watched within the familiar confines of Cameron Indoor Stadium. In one of the greatest basketball games of all time, Siren and I nestled inside our favorite hangout and dauntlessly watched the Blue Devils play until they sent their opponents crawling back home. I remember one Saturday night in March. In the small tobacco town of Durham, North Carolina, the street had grown quieter by the minute as fans and students quickly poured into nearby bars and restaurants. Siren and I were among those students who sped to Brightleaf Square, a short drive from East Campus. Inside the jam-packed restaurant bar, Evana, where I bought Siren her first shot of orgasm, waiters took turns running their cash registers and stealing glances at the large-screen TV. The announcer introduced the starting lineup from each team. A few stragglers wandered in and had no luck finding empty seats. Sitting shoulder to shoulder, some stuffed their mouths with pizzas and hamburgers. Other chunked down curly fries and onion rings. The rest gurgled down pitchers of beer.

"To the Blue Devils!" I cheered. I toasted Siren and those around me.

The tip-off began the game. The fierce battle between the two explosive teams sent hearts thumping. We wanted our enemies vanquished. We wanted them drooling in defeat. All game long, we watched our men in blue uniforms parry and be thwarted. They methodically chipped away their rivals' lead with succinct, fast-paced and remarkable passes, dribbles, and two- and three-point shots. We cracked our knuckles and gaped pop-eyed as the two teams fought aggressively over loose balls. The players dashed across the court. They slashed through lanes with thunderous jams. We bit our nails with lightning fast reflexes as the flawed, frayed, and desperately fought battle continued. With only a fraction of a minute left in overtime, all eyes in the room remained focused on our limping heroes. The defensive warriors huddled lethargically around their legendary head coach and headed back into the battlefield for a final offensive attack. We held our breath and gritted our teeth. The clock started ticking again. Droopy-eyed and emotionally exhausted, we exhibited a minimum preparation for what was about to happen next. Like a ticking time bomb ready to explode, we sat side by side, divided in hearts. Some thought that the game was over. The team had no chance of making a comeback. Others never doubted. Our demeanors reflected our beliefs.

The clock ticked closer to zero. A Blue Devil sprinted down the court. Another was left unguarded to throw the pass. The ball flew high across the court and corralled below the Spectrum scoreboard. Someone caught the ball at the foul line. The crowd hushed. With his back to a pair of defenders, the Blue Devil faked to the left, spun back, and launched a shot to the hoop. The buzzer went off. The shot was good! The ball miraculously swished through the net. The frustrated, sheepish, and frostbitten crowd in Evana transformed into a drunken brawl. Pandemonium electrified the restaurant bar. First came the chants, "Go, Devils, go!" Next came the hugs. Then came the high fives and party trumpet blares. Tinged with a sensation of relief and a renewed sense of urgency, some jumped into the air with fists pumping and gave an emphatic, "Yes!" Others stood and marveled at the sight of flying bodies.

The thrill of victory sent hundreds pouring out of bars and dormitory lounges, all storming across town to the heart of West Campus, where an inferno flared. Police patrolled all corners of the streets. Within minutes a crowd of nearly 3,000 revved-up fans engulfed the Clocktower Quad. It was party time inside the Gothic Wonderland. A cadre of delirious students ripped up a nearby bench and hurled it into the raging flames. Public safety officers armed with fire extinguishers stood ready to douse out the flares should things spin out of hand. Blasting boom boxes, spitting firecrackers, showering tennis balls, and streaming toilet papers engulfed the atmosphere. Women hoisted on male revelers' shoulders slathered themselves with beer and shaving cream.

"We want more! We want more!" the people chanted.

Responding to the crowds, women removed their brassieres, swung them around their heads, and tossed them into the conflagration. Loud cheers fired off. Men with blue-painted torsos, tan-line naked, raced around the scorching flame. Students pranced around like cult members in a devil-worshiping ceremony. They danced and leaped. Others climbed onto platforms near the sanctioned blaze. They splattered jugs of wine cooler on the crowd and charged closer to the flame.

With her back against the amber granite wall of House I, home of AEII, Siren grabbed me for a kiss. "We won, baby!" she exclaimed, chest rising and falling.

Chapter 7

ERUDITIO RELIGIO

LIFE AT THE UNIVERSITY was more than basketball campouts and Friday night keg parties. For Siren and me it was a time of personal growth and intellectual discovery. We filled our minds with information from books and theories and enlightened ourselves with psychology, chemistry, and philosophy. Whether around a dinner table, in a bar, or at the East Campus bus stop during noon rush hour, there never was a shortage of hot topics to discuss. We roamed the library reading rooms when term paper deadlines loomed and we panicked like everyone else in the midst of exams. We loved short lunches in quick snack bars and big dinners in fine dining halls. Although some of us were more willing than others to engage in intellectual debates or reflect on moral issues, we each had our own vision, and each was determined to push things to the limit. We meant no harm or disrespect to anyone. We simply did not know better.

Siren and I initiated ourselves into our new culture while trying to maintain our old ones. We found ourselves lost amid the different sets of rigidly enforced values and rules. In this process of change, our stories, symbols, and unique language gave life to a new self. Sometimes we found ourselves in fraternity and sorority rush scenes and keg parties. Other times we found ourselves in a heated class debates. Whatever we did and wherever we went, we remained vigilant. We changed our wardrobes in an attempt to blend in with the norm. We trimmed our hair to suit the image we tried to adopt. We tried to act cool and appeal to the opposite sex. Even our mannerisms and conversation styles changed. Our tone of voice and attitude varied from those portrayed at home. We became less constrained and more open.

When the holiday rolled around, we skillfully tucked away our newfound habits and transformed back into our old selves. Not until a slip of tongue provoked an awkward stare at the dinner table did we realize that those days of conservative restraint and naive civility had been washed offshore to some distant land. Once liberated, we found it impossible to reroute back to the old path. We could only sail onward into the high seas of the unknown as our ship of life shifted three hundred and sixty degrees. However fate twisted and turned, our views of the world and our views on life were never again the same. They evolved from generality and abstraction to particularity and objectivity.

Siren and I shaped and molded each other's views on life and love. Like many of our peers we had our ups and downs. One day we broke up, and the next day we got back together. Whatever our problems, we tried our best to cope with what we had. Whatever infinitesimal shred of happiness Siren deserved, I tried my best to give it to her. I also was the source of her heartaches and headaches.

Siren constantly struggled to strike a balance between her grades, her job and her time spent with me. She was an academic procrastinator. Sometimes she delayed school assignments for a day or two and sometimes a week or two. Foreseeable and unforeseeable circumstances forced her to push things back. Frequently she stormed into class half an hour late. Sometimes she did not bother to show up at all. When study period for mid-term or finals began, she could not care less how she looked or what she ate. Unlike me, who worried about how to top the other guy in class, she stressed over her survival for the upcoming grueling exam. The anticipated stress, the lack of sleep, the poor diet, and the changing weather took a toll on her body. Coughing, sneezing, sore throat; she had it all. She even fainted on her way to her recitation class. On the night before every exam, she paced nervously around my hardwood floor and threw questions at me left and right. When the big moment arrived, her mind shut down.

Whatever the circumstances that pushed Siren's schedule back, I was not at liberty to ask. Even when I did ask, I often received no answer. If there was one thing I learned early in our relationship, it was my obligation to abide by one rule: not to be nosy. I learned that to maintain civility in our relationship, I must never impinge upon her secrecy unless she chose to reveal something, and there were certain things she did not reveal.

One factor I know contributed to Siren's academic quagmire was her long work hours. Her dire financial situation required her to work after class and on weekends. Like everything else, longer work hours meant a shorter social life and less study time. That was her challenge, trying to juggle multiple tasks and be successful in all of them.

Siren needed the money. She was a woman who had everything and yet nothing. She had charm, beauty, intelligence, and a strong work ethic, but she lacked one essential element: money.

Money was the key to all things. It could lock and unlock doors. Without money, my life would have been miserable.

Although she rarely mentioned money or complained about her problems, I knew Siren was short of cash. She was and has always been short of cash. She did not have to tell me. I knew it from the clothes she wore and the shoes she purchased. They were not Armani, Gucci, or even J Crew, but clothes with generic names. There was nothing wrong with that. What she had on was neither flashy nor ugly. She did what she could with what she had.

I knew how bad Siren's financial crisis was at the time. Credit card companies hounded her daily. They called her in the morning, afternoon, and evening. She had no peace of mind. Her credit was so bad that no loan officer in his right mind would extend her more credit. Accompanying the persistent flood of phone calls were numerous dunning letters demanding payments. The letters grew from mild and inquisitive to hostile. Some even threatened legal action. What could she do? She could not give them what she did not have. She was only a poor college student who was trying to get through freshman year. All Siren wanted was an opportunity to live a dream, dream to receive a high-caliber education so that one day she would be treated with more respect. All she wanted was a chance to learn, so that someday she, too, could look people in the eye and say, "Hey, I did it. I survived. I can take whatever you throw at me, including your fancy words and pretentious manner."

A chance, by Siren's definition, meant something she earned. It meant something she could be proud of. It did not mean accepting charity from a generous boyfriend like me. Even if she had to live on canned foods for weeks at a time or work extra hours, she did it, to prove she could survive on her own. She did it so she would not have to smell another can of sardines. She did it for the sake of giving herself an opportunity to live the life she dreamed of living.

I frequently offered help, but she refused. Hardheaded and stubborn, Siren turned down my money every time. The temptation was high, but she held strong and looked the other way. Her rule of thumb was never to borrow or accept money from anyone, unless it was absolutely essential.

"You're my boyfriend, not my godfather or personal banker," Siren told me.

"That's ridiculous. Why are you letting your pride get in the way? There are much better things you can do with your time than work at your low-wage job." My words had no effect on her. Oddly, I respected her decision. She knew when to put her foot down and let reality throw punches at her. With each punch received, she bit her lip, got back up, and took another punch. I admired her. She was a true soldier. Inside her delicate appearance, an iron horse was hidden. I slowly figured her out as I watched her deal with each incoming blow.

Financial difficulty was not the only factor that contributed to Siren's problems. At the eye of the storm was me, Victor, the irresistible, irresponsible, and untrustworthy boyfriend. I allowed temptations to work on my weaknesses. The moment a beautiful girl flashed a smile at me, my clandestine activities began. My unfaithfulness was something I was not proud of. Neither was it something I could control. My unregulated behavior violated our most sacred contract. I breached the mutual trust between Siren and me. I was guilty because I was the ultimate player, intended or not. Siren, like many other unfortunate ones, fell for my cursed charm, good looks, and generosity. Crafty and gifted, I had a special talent for diffusing women's objectivity and working my way into their hearts. Those who believed they could mold me into the loyal type were in for a surprise. A predator on the prowl, taming me was impossible. It did not take long before Siren figured that out.

"Who is she?" Siren finally asked.

"Who's who?"

"Don't act dumb. I'm talking about the blonde you had dinner with last night in the University Room."

"She's just a friend," I lied, and I knew she knew. She could probably hear the blood in my veins rushing, see my pupils dilating, and smell my sweat. Who was I trying to fool? I should have known better. She was out of my league when it came to things like that. All her life she had been lied to. She was a pro at detecting lies.

"What kind of friend would put her arm around you-know-what?" she blurted.

"You're being paranoid."

"Am I?"

"We were just having dinner."

"Yeah, right."

"I'm telling you the truth."

"Stop lying, for Christ's sake! Lily told me everything."

I knew it. Lily would betray me in a heartbeat. I should have known better than to be physically involved with someone like her. A she-devil, Lily was the amicable, devious, and seductive type who would do whatever it takes to get her way, and she happened to be Siren's best friend. It should not have happened but it did; I slept with Lily. It happened when I went over to her place looking for Siren. What is a man to do when a half-naked girl approaches him in the heat of the night? Her long legs, her swelling bosoms, and her killer perfume rent me to pieces like the blows of buffalo horns. My body told me one thing and my mind another. In the end, my body won. Part of human nature and man's nature is to give in to lust. It was especially in my nature to give in to lust. The evolutionary process has ensured the continual propagation of man's genes for millions of years and will continue to ensure the existence of the human species for millions more to come. Whatever the reason, I still had no excuse to cheat on Siren, but I was nowhere near admitting my guilt. To admit my wrongdoing was to put myself at the mercy of her wrath.

"Lily said you slept with that woman," Siren said. "She also said you slept with several others down the hall. Did you or did you not?"

For a second my tongue stiffened, then the lie crept out. "I can't believe you actually believe that bitch. She's filling your head with unsubstantiated gossip."

"Why would she do such a thing? What does she have to gain?"

Again, I was struck speechless. I had reserved my attack on Lily in the past, but Lily had me cornered that time. I became the little squirrel with nowhere to run but straight ahead, where danger stood. Lily left me with no choice.

Vengeance was the answer. I hate to rat on other people, but I had to save myself first before drowning in the sea of lies. Siren had to hear the truth, whether she liked it or not.

"You have no idea who Lily is," I said. "That woman ought to be on every man's shit list. Do you know she came onto me the other night?"

Siren's eyes widened. I could tell she had not anticipated what I had to reveal. She looked angry and confused, but she remained resilient. "What do you mean she came onto you?"

"We had sex." I shut my eyes and prepared for the slap.

"You did what?" Siren spat.

"I was not thinking. I was looking for you, and instead I found her. She seduced me."

"Did she seduce you or did you simply throw your horny ass at her?"

I stepped back. "It doesn't matter."

"The hell it does! Why did you have to screw my best friend of all people?"

"I don't know. It wasn't supposed to happen. I'm sorry."

"Sorry isn't going to cut it."

"I told her it was a one-time deal." The truth was it happened. It happened even under Siren's watchful eyes. It happened not only with Lily but also with other women. I slept with one down the hall, two upstairs, several in a dorm across from mine, and so on, but they were only one-night stands. I could not help it. However good, honest, and loyal I tried to be, the bad seed in me was still there. I could not bring myself to confess, because the thought of losing Siren was not acceptable. She was the only woman I truly loved. I used others for sex, but not Siren. My relationship with Siren was different. She was more than a one-night-stand type of gal. She was an understanding friend, a soothing companion, a passionate lover, and the one who offered me spiritual guidance in my godless world. Utterly captivating, idealistic, and driven, she was the perfect match for me. Behind the girlish laugh and the wry exterior stood a woman of strength. She had endured the world's most brutal abuses, yet she held herself up.

As a privileged child from a wealthy family, I missed the opportunity to see things in their true light. Thanks to Siren, reality showed its true face. She unveiled a world I never knew existed. Her determination, her drive, and her will to survive in a tug-a-war struggle against the very force that held her back won my respect.

Given the trying circumstances I had put her through, Siren had threatened to end our relationship on more than one occasion, but it was a task more difficult to say than to do. Each time she spilled her anger and wanted to walk away, I used my charm to win her back. My charm worked every time and it worked with every woman. This ability to seduce women was both a blessing and a curse. It was a blessing because I could get whatever or whoever I wanted. I might have to put more effort in some cases than others, but in the end I normally got what I wanted. The charm was also a curse, because I could get whatever

and whomever I wanted. Such barnacles of unprece-
dented success spoiled a young consumerist mind.

"You remind me of a preacher I once knew," Siren said.
"Every Sunday he stood behind his pulpit and preached in
his self-righteous manner. After service he went inside his
private chamber and fucked the hell out of the choir girls."

Siren was right. I was a hypocrite, a seducer, and a liar,
but that did not deter her from staying with me. Torn
between love and hate, she became entangled in a web
that not even I could help her break. She loved how I
made her feel and hated how I lied and cheated. More
importantly, she did not like the social circle I belonged
to. "You're too rich for your own good and for society's
good," Siren said. "Thousands died each day from thirst
and hunger, and there you are, you and people like you,
squandering thousands away in fancy cars, big houses, and
expensive jewelry."

I knew Siren would not be happy in my world the
moment we entered my father's grand estate. On her first
visit to my house Siren's eyes followed the long curving
driveway that led to two black Mercedes parked on one
side of the house. We strolled past a wooden bridge that
overlooked a pond filled with color-splotched fish.
Caught between awe and trepidation she was reluctant to
move closer to a gigantic timber door guarded by two
stone soldiers on horseback. She appeared to be fear of
meeting my father, a man of great discipline but few
words. She probably felt that he would never accept her,

not because she lacked intelligence, common courtesy, or good looks, but because she lacked proper breeding.

I rang the bell. The door cracked to show a tall and handsomely built man with steel-gray hair, chiseled jaw, squared shoulders, and quiet demeanor.

"You must be Siren," my father said, reaching out for a firm handshake.

"Yes, I'm Siren, sir," Siren quavered.

"Please come in."

Siren and I stepped inside and trailed my father to the guestroom. It was a large room of European-style architecture. The marble rotunda crowned by a Spanish-tiled dome held an aura of quiet power that struck even Siren's nerves. She seemed tamed by the enormity of the place. Her eyes studied the meticulously painted ceilings, the pillared corridor, and the giant glass vaults. She marveled at the swords, the battle drums, the guns, and the black-and-white photos on the wall. They were pictures of military men in uniform, government officials, and familiar faces of foreign diplomats and powerbrokers. Siren took it all in.

"How come you never told me your father is in the military?" she whispered.

"You never asked." Yes, my father was a military man and a highly decorated soldier. He ranked among the best. He was a four-star general, to be exact. Ambitious, politically savvy, and intellectually gifted, my father made his way up the power ladder quicker than any man I knew. Since the age of seventeen, when he made the decision to attend West Point, my father was destined for greatness. Somewhere between the classrooms of West Point and the National War College, and the battlefields of Vietnam and North Korea, a general was born. It was in my father's blood to be a military man, and a military man he was. My father did not take lightly any amusing comments about his rank, reputation, or possessions.

Siren made one such comment about his favorite sedan chair, and he was offended. I honestly believe that the failure of communication on my part had brought about the failure of a forthright and cordial relationship between my father and Siren. Whatever words that were exchanged between the two while I stepped aside to the kitchen to make tea, that day was the first and last time Siren stepped foot into my house.

Chapter 8

SOMETHING MAGICAL

LL IN ALL FRESHMAN YEAR was a year of magic and a year of wonder. It was a perfect time in an imperfect world for two aspiring young minds. When the leaves turned gold and littered the ground, Siren and I took mile-long strolls down Campus Drive. On cloudless nights we visited Observation Park and watched the planes speed off under the star filled sky. After an evening shower, Siren and I went out for a short drive. We went like two crazy kids down the tree-covered tunnel of University Drive. There was nothing else to do in a small town like Durham at such an hour of the night but study, sleep, drive, or have sex. All the shops were closed, and the only things in sight for miles were the trees, the woods, and the red traffic lights that refused to turn green. Thump, thump, thump, water droplets fell off trees and tapped Pixie's tin roof as we zoomed down University Drive. Pixie, Siren's two-door hatchback, was a cranky mechanical horse with a gnawed-up engine for a brain. She gave up on us once in the middle of the night. Black smoke surged out of her tailpipe and billowed sky high. Siren and I ran out of Pixie and dove for the ground. Lucky for us, a tanker truck driver with a fire extinguisher arrived.

If autumn was great, winter was comforting. On frosty mornings Siren and I woke up early to enjoy the view of the snow-covered quad. On cold winter nights we critiqued and created arts. Siren was the art connoisseur, and I was the artist. She admired my gift to create multi-hued transparency and illusionary effects, and I admired her ability to share her thoughts on such transparency and illusionary effects. Whether behind the Duke Chapel walls, in a boxed corner of Lilly Library's basement, in the art studio, or in my dormitory room, there were just the two of us and shielded from the world, reading, studying, and making art. We spent sundry evenings examining the daunting works of Van Gogh, Monet, Renoir, de Breanski, da Vinci, and Bierstadt.

On a prickly December night, under a full moon, Siren posed nude. Statuesque and rippling with an irrepressible vitality, she lay before me on my bed wearing nothing but a diamond necklace. Her dark hair, satin skin, columnar legs, and swimmer's waist must have been the handiwork of her sculptor God. That night, Siren was mine to observe, mine to appreciate, and mine to immortalize.

I painted her while she studied my drawings on the wall. They were pictures of a man painting a woman in the center of a mystical room interspersed within twenty transitional pieces.

Siren and I packed our bags and headed for Daytona Beach when spring and its warmer weather arrived. We chose Daytona for its long shoreline, its large waves, its diverse crowds, and its accessibility. Accessibility was important for Siren and me. Daytona was the only place we knew that we could drive Pixie down to the shoreline and enjoy a good tan. Having Pixie right there by our side was practical. Everything was within reach. If we wanted sparkling water, Pixie had it. If we wanted watermelons, Pixie had it. If we wanted hip-hop, pop, or country music, Pixie also delivered. Pixie was like home. In fact, she was our mobile home. Although I had a better car, Siren insisted on using Pixie. Pixie went everywhere we went. We enjoyed her company, and she enjoyed ours. That was all that mattered to Siren and me.

It was a good day's drive to Daytona Beach. Siren and I took turns at the wheel dodging hot-tempered drivers with U-haul trailers, hillbillies in motor homes, and sleep-deprived truckers in eighteen-wheelers. Whatever we did, we were always on the lookout for old folks. More specifically, we kept our eyes open at all costs to screen for old folks in large cars on the road. No matter how innocent they looked, old folks behind the wheel were the most dangerous type. For some odd reason, they loved the fast lane. They drove at a snail's pace in the fast lane. It was a mystery to me why these elderly loved the fast lane. Maybe the far left lane was the least distracting lane to be in, or maybe knowing they could drive fast in that lane excited them. They knew they could not drive fast without endangering themselves and the lives of others, though. They knew they had bad eyes, horrible hearing, and slow reflexes. They also knew they had frail backs, but they held onto the fast lane anyway, for all the life in them. They camped in the lane as if they owned it. They acted as if they had easement rights, and they drove slower than a tortoise, going twenty in a fifty-five-mile-an hour lane. Far ahead, we could barely see their head full of white hair protruding above the steering wheel. Three quarters of a mile later, their heads expanded in size, and so did the size of their cars. They grew until Siren or I either steered right or faced the unavoidable consequences, a deadly collision into the bumper of their two-ton steel machine. If a collision did occur, they would live to see us die. Pixie would not have stood a chance against her armored adversaries. She would have been crushed into a thin metallic piece and Siren and I would have been sandwiched in between.

Siren called those old folks' cars supertankers. I called them boats of steel. The old folks did not mess around when it came to safety. They knew they had bad backs; therefore they went out and purchased the biggest, bawdiest, and hardest piece of equipment they could find. Siren and I avoided the elderly at all costs, and because of our extra precaution, we lived to see Daytona Beach.

Siren and I celebrated our arrival at Daytona with a quick toast of Armenian cognac and went out for a pleasure drive down Atlantic Avenue. High-hormone college students packed the night street. Everyone had one goal in mind, a good time. Women in bikinis flaunted themselves. Red, white, and black convertibles crawled up the road. BMWs, Cadillacs, Mercedes, Fords and Harley Davidsons lined bumper to bumper. Siren and I bathed in the energy, the livelihood, and the sensuality of the moment. We stayed up late and woke up early. We explored the jumble of modern condos and vintage clothing stores. We roamed the late-night bars and techno clubs. We walked the sugary shoreline, basked under the scorching sun, and surfed the choppy waves. When we were hungry we feasted on chili prawns until we could barely move. We hung out at cocktail lounges and stay-out-late cafes. We ordered martinis and sank into the world of leisurely pleasure. When all was done, we drove back to the place we both called home, my cozy little room with a walk-in closet in the small town of Durham, North Carolina.

Chapter 9

SWEET ADIEU

OUR DAYS TOGETHER at the university were brief but sweet. The temperature climbed, the wind picked up speed, and the night faded into day. The sprinkling summer haze replaced the crescent moon and a billion glowing stars. The realization struck Siren and me one morning that another chapter of our lives had come to a close. Shelves were emptied, classrooms vacated, and food courts hollowed out. Squirrels and birds replaced the curious wanderers and sun-hungry students that once occupied the quad. Inside each dormitory and adjacent to every door, class notes and empty pizza boxes packed the hall.

The eerie atmosphere reminded Siren and me that our freshman year had finally come to an end. Despite our relieved anticipation, we felt lonely to be two of the few left on campus. Pothead, my oddball of a neighbor who frequently threw late-night parties, was also one of those rare few who remained. His harmonica echoed vibrantly from the other side of the wall. The night before, he sat cross-legged under the sky at the heart of East Campus quad staring into the stars. When he saw me passing by, he exchanged a polite nod and returned to his meditative state.

Siren and I too had our soul-searching moment. It was one enduring year. From relationship troubles to financial crisis and academic turmoil, we faced them all. Sometimes they were self-imposed and sometimes they were not. Those were the memorable times of our youth. The vacant campus reminded us that all good and bad times must come to an end, including the constant commotion; Thursday night poker games; and Friday night dinners at the Blue Cow, a restaurant known for its elephant-size waitresses, limitless country-style barbecue, and bad service. Who could forget the foul-smelling anchovy pizza, stale odors of freshman vomit on our door, annoying prank phone calls, and resounding fraternity clamors?

Some weeks we slept during the day and partied at night, leaving limited time for studying. Other weeks we studied during the day and into the night, leaving little room for partying. Whatever our habits were, there were always the intellectual debates, the basketball celebrations that lasted until who knows when, and the memorable sex in the closet on rainy nights. Regardless of what elements that drove Siren and me apart, sex always brought us back

together. Occasionally, we stayed up multiple nights having sex. After sex, Siren gathered her undergarments,
slipped into her favorite blue jeans, and quietly left my
room. I would not hear from her again for days until her
urge returned.

Part III

TIME TO REND

Brooklyn 1992

Chapter *10*

DAMN YANKEES

THREE DAYS AFTER FINALS, Siren and I cleared our refrigerators; trashed our notes; sped out of Durham, North Carolina; and rushed up to New York City. Why New York City? Well, it was Siren's hometown, a place where she grew up and a place where she wanted me to visit before our cross-country trip to Stillwater, Minnesota. I had always wanted to see the Big Apple but never took the chance. I was a southern boy living in a southern town who did not care to venture anywhere farther north than the Mason-Dixie line. It was sad but true. I had traveled the world but never visited a city I had so much admired.

I had climbed the Great Wall of China, walked the streets of Paris, skied the Alps, and dined in the finest Swiss cafés, but I had never set foot on Broadway or Fifth

Avenue. Something about New York City must have driven me off all those years. Maybe I was scared of its humongous size and multi-layered underground tunnels and passageways. I heard many horror stories about the city, tales of tourists being mugged by underground people, pick-pocketed by starving panhandlers, or pushed to death in front of a moving subway train by a vengeful crowd. Above the ground, there were the honking Yellow Cabs, screaming taxi drivers, deafening police-car and fire-truck sirens, and unforgiving boombox noises that filled the streets of Times Square.

"Those damn Yankees. They're rude, obnoxious, impatient, and loud. Why should I have to put up with them when I don't have to?" Those were my excuses to stay away. Whatever the reason might have been, I managed to stay away from the crossroad of the world for many years. I received numerous invitations to wedding parties, Broadway shows, and even New Year's celebrations, but I turned them all down and continued to imagine what the city was like. In my mind, New York City was larger than life. It was a giant anthill filled with arteries of lights. I rode past the city once at the age of five on one of the long family road trips to Boston that I vaguely recall. That was enough, that is, until I met Siren. She convinced me otherwise, that a man like me should not hide in a small town like Durham, North Carolina, a town where tobacco was grown and where squirrels run free.

"You must get over your fear and pay the Big Apple a visit," she said.

"What fear?" I rebutted, but Siren was right. I did fear the great city of New York. Its name alone shook the very foundation of my world. I realized that I was just another sheltered small-town guy who looked and acted tough. Deep inside, I was just a little boy hiding from Godzilla.

Throughout the school year, Siren told me so much about the city that never sleeps. She talked about the Italians, the Chinese, the Russians, and the Koreans. She talked about Broadway, Wall Street, and Fifth Avenue. She talked about the Brooklyn Bridge, the Empire State Building, and the Twin Towers. She talked about Chelsea Pier, SoHo, Little Italy, and Chinatown. She even talked about Canal Street, once covered with water, but now a flourishing and bustling street where exotic fruits and vegetables were sold. She gave me vivid details of the Upper East Side, the Upper West Side, Central Park, and the East and West Villages. Gradually, my unease for New York City dissipated as she shared more about its lobster houses, sports bars, restaurants, pizzerias, and coffee joints littered with grown men and women deep in conversation. What struck me most were the tales of her legendary boat rides across the Hudson to Staten Island. Along these tales came the names and history of the many vessels that have served as a main source of transportation between the two boroughs for nearly two centuries.

"People started crossing the Hudson between Staten Island and Manhattan in the early 1700s," Siren said. "The steamboat service started a century later." Then came the names of the three-hundred-something-foot ferries that looked like giant ladybugs from the distance. I learned about the pre-1905 Southfield, Westfield, and Clifton followed by stories of the past President Roosevelt, Gold Star Mother, Knickerbocker, and Miss New York.

On a windswept Sunday morning, Siren took the subway train from Brooklyn to Battery Park City. From there she caught the next boat at Whitehall Ferry Terminal across the Hudson to Staten Island. "It was a nice boat ride across the river," Siren said. "When the boat pulled out into the harbor from Battery Park, it provided a perfect vintage view of lower Manhattan's majestic skyline receding and a great view of the industrial New Jersey docks." As the ferry hurried southwest across the five-mile-wide river and passed in between Ellis Island and Liberty Island on one side and Governor's Island on the other, Siren pulled out her coffee mug and sugar-glazed donut and enjoyed a simple breakfast while the cool breeze brushed by.

"Things felt different early that morning," Siren said. "There was an inner calm in seeing the red sun edging up the horizon, flaring the darkened water, and meticulously painting the world with its trillion hair thin-brushes." According to her, the sun colored the sailboats, tugboats, cruise ships, barges, and oil tankers. Its rays sprayed the pointy domes of Ellis Island and raced next door, an island over, to wrap Lady Liberty with its light. Seagulls circled the boat with wings spread and beaks open, readied at all times to snatch at anything she threw at them. The birds swirled left and right, floating weightlessly and paralleling the moving boat. They rode the air with their big white wings. At a moment's notice they plunged from the sky on a kamikaze dive. One by one they extracted the falling breadcrumbs with pinpoint precision and swirled back up just before crashing into the testy water inches below.

Twenty-five minutes later, at Saint George Ferry Terminal, the orange Andrew J. Barberi banged to a stop. Shaken awake not by the coffee that she drank but by the unsuccessful docking of an inexperienced Sunday morning captain, Siren stood waiting for the boat to fully align. "Keep off ramp until Ferryboat is fast to dock," the overhead sign read. Siren ignored such a sign. So did everyone else. Left and right, the boat banged. It continued to steer and plow into the enormous wooden pilings. The boat cried of raw steel grinding against wood as it skewed to the pier. Left and right, the passengers jostled.

After a few trials of heading and butting, the captain finally got it right. The boat aligned straight on with the slip and locked still. A few sleepy onlookers peeked beyond the tip of their baseball caps and hinted a nod of approval to the inexperienced captain. Others stepped aside to let the landing crew clear the safety rope. A head above a bridge lowered. Its pulley chains squeaked against the revolving reels. The loud noises then fettered to a stop.

Siren wasted no time scurrying off the boat. She raced ahead of the crowd, cut through the bus tube platform and headed for Richmond Terrace. She jogged passed the deli and Mini Market, Staten Island Police Station, and

Family Court, and veered left at the corner of Richmond Terrace and Hamilton Avenue. Head lowered and shoulders squared she made her way up hill on the near vertical climb. The hill leveled off at the crossing of Saint Mark's Place. Siren turned right and began her decline. She raced down the swirling road and passed the multicolored gingerbread-shaped houses. Straight ahead at the edge of the hill overlooking the water, St. Peter's R.C. Church towered before her eyes, its long steeple pinned to the sky with a round clock near the top and a white cross at its peak. Tracing the church wall toward the bottom, a granite stairway zigzagged in a near vertical drop. Behind its vanishing point were the Hudson, the red cargo ships on the Hudson, and the distant Manhattan skyline. Siren treasured the view.

Chapter II

FLIGHTS OF FURY

S IREN'S IDEALISTIC VIEW of New York City
quickly faded when we pulled into her neighborhood. It was a wild place she lived in, worse than a
zoo, and a total war zone. I could not imagine living in
such a place. It felt like something out of a movie. Graf-
fiti filled walls, and bullet holes riddled doors. Half-fallen
cyclone fences had been pried with head size holes. Chairs
and desks were thrown out of windows. Bookshelves, old
lamps, broken TVs, and filthy garbage bags rotted with
sour vegetables lined the street. Sidewalks cracked, and
manholes welted. Loud music blasted through car windows and doors. The people, they were just as scary.

Gangs of teens with gold teeth and wearing bandanas
stared us down from their yards as Siren and me inched
closer to Siren's home. Wild-eyed seniors rocked away on

their front porch while their younger counterparts fought behind open doors. Children, half-naked and unsupervised, circled the spraying fire hydrants and screamed, hollered, and chased each other. I felt stressed just looking at the place. I had no idea that Siren lived in such an environment; neither had I a clue how she could have survived and even flourished in such a place. My only explanation was simple: adaptation. People adapted to the environment where they lived. Some were born into it, and others were forced into it. Whatever the case, man had done it for years. People adjusted, changed, and adapted.

Most of the folks in Siren's neighborhood adapted by turning to those in control. Those in control were no angels. They were drug pushers, child abusers, violent perpetrators, pimps, and thugs. Homicides, intimate-partner violence, sexual assaults, and youth gang wars were part of life in that ecologically unsound niche. Was prostitution a way for a poor young woman like Siren to survive? It appeared likely, from the look of things. Had Siren sold her body in exchange for food and money? I dared not ask, but I suspected that she did what she had to do to survive.

Although a frequent church attendee, Siren was not exactly the innocent type. She was a maverick with many faces that had mastered concealing her true state of mind. With Siren, she believed in living the moment and not questioning her past. Whether I wanted to or not, I learned to accept her for the way she was and what she had to offer. What she had to offer was joy one moment and grief and befuddlement the next. I accepted her because she had the courage to shamelessly haul me into her potholed neighborhood controlled by gangs and thugs. She might not be rich by society's standard, but she was rich by mine. She was rich with strength, bravery, and a will to survive.

Siren stopped Pixie at the front of a two-story brick apartment complex that leaned against a smoke-colored sky. The sound of a pistol fired off. I ducked like an ostrich. A loud screech followed as a black Prelude sped out of the parking lot. "Relax." Siren laughed. "No one is shooting at you. If someone wanted you killed, you'd be dead by now."

I felt betrayed by my cowardly act. I, Victor, the son of a great American general, had ducked before a girl I was supposed to protect. With frequent sidelong glances, I stepped out of the car and followed Siren upstairs to her house. She opened the door. A rude awakening awaited Siren inside. Emptied beer bottles, stale chip crumbs, and cigarette butts scattered the floor. Wild odors and collected dust choked the air.

Stretched on the living room couch with a foot on the musty brown carpet was a burly, Stalin-like man. Unshaven and subdued by the alcohol he had drunk, the man anchored immobile on the couch. I could not make out whether he was looking at us or staring past Siren and me. His eyes, lifeless and stone cold, gazed our way. It must be the incoming fresh air that stirred his sense, or perhaps it was the traffic noises from outside. A few feet away, the TV flickered. The news was on. A black line cut the screen in halves and oscillated horizontally. The old TV sported a crooked antenna, poor resolution, and garbled sound, but it still served its purpose. It inhibited the mind of the man on the couch and brightened the shadowy room where he lay.

"Jesus Christ!" Siren cried. "Look at this mess!" She sped past the man and scurried into her room.

I felt Siren's pain. I suspected she had a troubled home life, but I did not know it was this bad. No wonder she always seemed distant. It explained why she had been reluctant to disclose her past. A part of her was lost. I thought I went through some hard times in my life, but they were nothing compared to hers. Siren went through far worse. No word could do justice to describe what I saw. I did not know what I had avoided until then. Right there and then, things finally cleared up. I knew I was blessed. Unlike Siren or Jack, I was spared from the cursed place Siren called home.

Jack was the son of Joe, the old man next door. Siren had a fling with Jack once, at the age of fifteen. She was young, and he was reckless. The whole thing was an accident, a Saturday night accident when Joe was out of town. Siren was standing in the back porch watching the stars, and Jack was on his way out to go wherever he was going. They met. A conversation ensued, touches exchanged, Jack's door re-opened, and clothes came off. Jack must have roughened Siren up that night. He must have greased her up on his kitchen floor, because it appeared he made a lasting impression on her. "Things got awkward afterward," Siren said. "For one, Jack already had a girlfriend he truly loved. Second, he was not my type. I did it because I was curious. He did it because he was a man. We both felt betrayed, not by each other or by ourselves, but by the damn summer heat."

Although Jack lived next door, Siren claimed that she did not know much about him until the FBI questioned her. He slept during the day and disappeared at night. Not even Joe knew the real Jack. Joe had no idea where Jack went each night or what kind of people he associated with. All Joe knew was his Jack, the dutiful son with a knife scar on the face. Jack paid the bills and put food on the table, and that was enough for Joe. There was an oddity about Jack that had drawn Siren to him at first. It was the darker side of him like the spectral night he roamed. Was Jack a member of the mob? The answer was yes, as Siren later found out. He was a member of the Russian mob. Jack was part Italian and part Russian and spoke both tongues. His father, Joe, was an Italian, and his mother a Russian. Whichever group he joined, Jack could fit right in. He was a natural when it came to hustling people. Jack had a way with words that could persuade the devil to yield. His charisma, his skill to instill fear in people, and his ability to remain inconspicuous to the outside world made Jack the perfect candidate for a life in organized crime.

The police and FBI questioned Siren about Jack's mob-related activities not long after her affair with him on that hot summer night. Whether in a shady Brooklyn street, a fancy restaurant in the Bronx, or a high profile Manhattan nightclub, Jack did his things—drug trafficking, blackmailing, and money laundering. The court finally issued a warrant for his arrest. More than a dozen officers were seriously injured in the intense crossfire when the police squad stormed into a nightclub where Jack and his crew worked. Shortly after Jack's arrest, he grabbed a gun from a lock box in an area where inmates were moved and escaped the city jail. The cops chased him across the borough but lost him in the end.

Jack was too good for the cops. He knew every hole and crevice in the Brooklyn neighborhood. He also knew the right people who would go the extra mile to protect him at all costs. He remained out of sight for weeks at a time. Rumor had it that the mob boss assigned him to do clerical work, temporary clerical work, Siren presumed, until the attention died down. The Feds might have eyes and ears, but Jack had better ones. From the time he woke up to the time he went to bed, Jack never ceased listening or stopped looking. If he could not do it himself he had other people do it for him. Jack did what he did for a living because it was what he could do best, and what he could do best involved outsmarting his enemies on all three fronts, the law enforcers, his rival mobs, and a guilty conscience. Winning the fight required a clear mind, a vigilant ear, and a watchful eye.

Only one thing in the world Jack could not control, the meddling hand of fate. Months after his escape, a mob gathering convened inside Mean Dean, a Staten Island restaurant. Members from the Los Angeles, Chicago, and New York crime families attended. A hired gunman guarded the door. At a quarter past midnight, a dispute broke loose. A shooting spree followed. Jack shot another mob boss in the head. By the end of the night, only the dead remained. Two days following the Staten Island mob massacre, Jack was gunned down in the street. Eyewitnesses saw him crawling in an attempt to escape, before being hauled off in broad daylight. One bystander described three white males in their early thirties fleeing the scene in a white van.

Chapter 12

FOOTHILLS OF THE
CARPATHIANS

S IREN'S REVELATION ABOUT JACK took me
by surprise. Whatever the reason might have been
that had held her back since the day we met, it was
about time she opened the door to her personal life. I had
waited long enough and deserved some explanation. Our
past discussions were merely past discussions. They were
all related to the state of mind at that time. We talked
about the weather. We talked about arts. We talked about
sports. We talked about wars and politics, but we never
talked about her intimate past. I could touch her, kiss her,
hug her, and make her squirm, but the wall remained
impenetrable, and the door into her mind stayed shut.
Strapped with locks and chains, that door was her power
over me. For the first time in nearly a year, Siren unveiled
another part of her life that I always wanted to know.

The daughter of a Russian artisan, Siren was born in a small house in the picturesque city of Lviv, a city of striking Baroque and Renaissance architecture located by the foothills of the Carpathians. Lviv, the City of Lions, was a city mentioned in the Volyn chronicle. It was named after its founder's heir, Leo, son of Galycian King Danylo Galytsky. There was a strip of land near Siren's house where her mother used to grow vegetables and an apple orchard where Siren used to play. For centuries, her ancestors had lived within the narrow confines of the city walls and walked its cobblestone streets. Some were merchants; others were craftspeople; and the rest were secular or religious gentry. They were the knife grinders, seamstresses, chimney sweeps, masseurs, chefs, slaughter-house workers, fishmongers, butchers, icemen, carpenters, street photographers, welders, sculptors, and shoemakers. For generations, the Greek Orthodox churches played a vital role in the religious lives of the citizen of Lviv and in the lives of Siren's family and predecessors, including those of her mother, grandmother, and great grandmother.

Siren was the first in her family to shift away from the deeply rooted Greek Orthodox tradition. It took a several-thousand-mile journey across the North Atlantic to make the change. Aspiring to make a better life for their only daughter, Siren's parents shipped her overseas to America in a cargo container at the tender age of six. Siren, formerly known as Katerina in the Ukraine, was given a different identity and a different name. She was renamed Siren for her incredible pure voice. Sirens, according to Greek mythology, were creatures with the head of a woman and the body of a bird who drew sailors toward their death on a craggy shoreline. According to myth, three sirens, daughters of Phorcus or Achelous, inhabited an island surrounded by dangerous rocks. They sang so enchantingly that sailors who heard them were drawn near and shipwrecked on the jagged coast. That was the power of a siren, my Siren, the power to enchant men and the power to seduce them.

Chapter 13

HOUSE OF
SHATTERED DREAMS

L IFE IN AMERICA was no apple pie. Siren lived
with her uncle Nikolai and his wife Anna in their
congested two-bedroom apartment in the poorest
part of Brooklyn. It was a neighborhood where migrant
workers and refugees dwelled. The apartment was about
the size of a feed barn, a feed barn that housed rodents,
flies, and roaches. Roaches were everywhere. When darkness took its toll and the light switched off, they crept out
by the hundreds and swamped the walls, the ceilings, and
the floor. They even crawled out of the cabinets and
closet doors. They popped beneath Siren's feet when she
walked barefoot in the dark, and they crawled over her
face or dropped into her mouth from the ceiling, when
she was sound asleep. Anna did everything within her
power to keep those bugs under control, but thanks to the

unsanitary habits of the occupants downstairs, the roaches multiplied. For each one killed, ten more were born. They invaded the kitchen floor in battle formation. Resistant to the roach poison, they marched onward with white-powdered heads and antennae.

On top of the flies, the rats, and the roaches, the summer heat made it unbearable to sleep at night. The only air conditioner in the house was the one installed in the living-room window. When July arrived, Anna, Nikolai, and Siren escaped to the foldout couch.

It was no five-star hotel that Siren lived in. Holes filled the walls, and cracked paint peeled from the ceiling. The plumber was never around when the kitchen sink drain clogged or the toilet failed to flow. To get things done, Anna had to do the job herself. She might have been small and thin, but when it came to getting things fixed around the house, she was Olive with Popeye's arms. "Don't let her size fool you," Siren said. "You should have seen her at work. Sleeves rolled up, elbows up, and feet steady on a stool, Anna pumped away. She worked the rubber plunger like an oil-drilling machine until the last drop of clog cleared."

There were some flaws in the house that not even Anna could fix. They included the loud noises and the clustered space, to name two. The width of the passageway connecting the living room to the two bedrooms was so narrow that tripping and falling over in its constricted confine would not be a pleasant experience for a big guy like Nikolai. He would be trapped with both elbows locked between the walls. A thornier problem involved the lack of a barrier between the living room and the formidable kitchen. The cold air in the winter, hot air in the summer, and musty air in the spring, in combination with a missing stovetop vent made every pre-meal wait a daunting task. In addition to the unforgiving weather and the free-floating oil and sauce particles from the frying pan that adhered to hair and clothes, there was the roaring window fan. "Although it partially served its purpose by sucking some of the smell out of the kitchen," Siren said, "it was obnoxiously loud."

The fan, among a list of other important household goods, was an item Anna handpicked from the neighborhood yard sales. Anna was the yard-sale queen. Her "Yardar," as Siren coined it, remained alert twenty-four seven. No woman in the neighborhood could outmatch Anna when it came to relaying information about an upcoming yard sale. She was the first to know and usually the first to spread the news. Other women depended on her. She had her system wired. Every phone line in the neighborhood channeled through hers. Anna would not miss a yard sale for the world. She would forego PTA meetings, skip teacher student conferences, and even bypass church services, but never forego a yard sale. She would go to one even if she did not have another dime to spend. Her odd obsession was her hallmark and something she was proud of. At least she had something to be proud of. Not many women in the neighborhood had such a privilege. Vanity kept Anna sane in the cruel world where she dwelled. It gave her hope and ensured her a sense of purpose, something she could look forward to each new day.

Anna's parsimonious reputation preceded the bad rumors that followed. Women in the neighborhood nicknamed her Anna the Scavenger, Anna the Bag Woman, or whatever names they could think of, but it did not matter. Neither Nikolai nor Siren paid much attention to the insults. What Anna did was good for the family. Her tireless efforts put extra food on the table. There was cotton candy for Siren; ripe mangoes for Nikolai; and fresh meats, breads, and potatoes for all three.

Thanks to Anna, Siren received her first telescope at the age of nine, a rare and priceless item. Anna got the perfectly useable telescope at a bargain price. It was in top-notch shape and had been sitting in a retired astronomer's closet collecting dust for years. Immediately after his death, his in-laws, not people of science, auctioned everything off, including the old telescope. "One man's loss is another woman's gain," Siren said. The telescope brought Siren a step closer to her true passion, studying the stars. It also brought her closer to her so-called God. It opened up a universe that her naked eyes could not see and unveiled its vast wonders beyond the fuzzy images from the Discovery Channel of her living room TV. Stars and galaxies she never knew existed were hers to grasp. The concept was bigger than her young imagination could grasp. With her very own telescope, Siren and Buddy, a playmate who lived next door, stayed up late on clear summer nights and studied the stars. They spun the telescope 360 degrees and enjoyed the panoramic view of the sky from the comfort of Siren's back porch.

Chapter 14

THE BOY NEXT DOOR

B UDDY LIVED A FLOOR BELOW in a separate apartment complex. He was the son of Mr. Schmidt, a local theater manager, and Mrs. Schmidt, a plump, gentle lady quiet in nature and a devoted Christian who ran a small grocery store a block down the road. Mrs. Schmidt always treated Siren like a daughter. She wished she had a daughter of her own. Unfortunately, following Buddy's birth, Mrs. Schmidt had been unsuccessful in conceiving another child.

When Siren was little, Mrs. Schmidt routinely brought her fresh bananas and strawberries each week. She also took Siren out for ice cream. In return, Siren accompanied her to church when Sunday rolled around. Anna did not mind that Siren tagged along. She, too, was a Methodist. As long as Siren was out of the house, Anna was happy. She needed the time to be alone and wished to be free from the burden of caring for another's child. It was not Anna's choice that Siren came under her care. Nikolai brought it upon her.

On Sunday afternoon, a week before each Christmas, Mrs. Schmidt, Buddy, and Siren gathered in a small room adjoining the congregation hall for their annual potluck dinner. There the Sunday school children reenacted The Birth of Christ. Siren was in the play once when she was seven, her second Christmas in America. She was shy and spoke limited English, but other kids did not mind. They liked her because she was cute. The adults also adored her because she was well behaved.

"Isn't she a doll?" Mrs. Schmidt often bragged and held on to Siren as if Siren was her own. Siren did not mind. She liked the attention. A child need love, whether from her own mother, from a strange woman, or from kids thousands of miles away from home. To obtain love, she learned to employ her assets, which were her long dark hair, her fair complexion, her full lips, and her adorable green eyes. Occasionally, she threw people a smile to win them over.

Siren learned the art of seduction at a young age, because it was her tool of survival. She had no parents, because her mother and father were an ocean away. When she cried in the darkest hours of the night, they could not hear her. They were not there to wipe her tears or tuck her back into bed with a bedtime story. She considered them dead. She buried them with the memories of her past in a distant world where she once lived. She welded her heart, controlled her emotions, and pretended to be happy.

Mrs. Schmidt, also a Sunday school teacher, had the perfect role for Siren, the role of the Virgin Mary. Mary was a gentle woman, and Siren was a gentle child; therefore, it was a perfect match. Playing Mary allowed Siren to conceal her lack of command for the new language she was beginning to learn. All she had to do was to carry a cardboard box with a baby Jesus doll and let the boys do all the talking.

On Christmas night, Mrs. Schmidt and Siren, along with other children in the church choir, assembled in a mini van and drove from house to house singing "Silent Night." The tradition was to make the final stop at the pastor's house.

Mrs. Schmidt always reminded Siren that she had a lovely voice, the voice of a little angel. Praise added warmth to Siren's heart, encouraged her growth, and reassured Siren that it was okay to sing, even if her English was not fully correct. After all, she was only a child, a child from a foreign land who spoke a foreign tongue.

"That night," Siren recalled, as I gazed into her eyes, "the trees, windows, and roofs of every house in the neighborhood lit up and blinked with colorful lights. The pastor, wearing his customary red shirt, brown suit, and a neck chain with a two-inch gold cross, stood quietly next to his wife and listened to us sing. Behind them was a tall, white Christmas tree embellished with red flowers and majestic gold angels. A brilliant star sat at the top. It was the most beautiful thing I had ever seen."

Chapter 15

BUDDY WAS NO SAINT

S IREN KNEW BUDDY FOREVER. They grew up in the same neighborhood, went to the same grade school, and attended the same junior high. They spent hours together behind Buddy's house watching cars and trucks go by. Sweet as he might have been to Siren, Buddy was no saint. He was a regular rebel in school. In third grade, he bullied the second graders, and in fourth grade, he picked on the third graders. In seventh grade Buddy flung a piece of meatball across the lunch table and stained the polka dot shirt of a sixth grade girl. The girl walked up to him, smacked him on the back of his head, and ran to the restroom with spaghetti sauce dripping down her back.

Once eighth grade rolled around, Buddy found himself another victim, Mr. Jones. Mr. Jones, or Santa, as Buddy called him, was a cross-eyed jolly old man with steely gray hair and a belly the size of a water barrel. Mr. Jones taught pre-algebra until Buddy and his troublemaking gang drove him to an early retirement. For twenty years Mr. Jones ran with an iron fist the math department of James Madison Junior High in Brooklyn. One day in the middle of a lecture, he walked out and was never heard from again.

Siren was not surprised that Mr. Jones quit. Buddy and his boys used to throw eggs at him while he taught class. They waited until the old man faced the chalkboard. When the coast was clear, Buddy and the boys launched their attack from outside. The raw eggs splattered all over him and the chalkboard. Mr. Jones flared with rage each time.

Buddy was the type of guy every teacher hated and most kids loved. He was the envy of those who wanted to rebel against authority but feared the consequences. His reputation among his peers solidified during his second year of junior high. On a hot Friday afternoon a week before summer break, a juvenile delinquent pushed Buddy off his seat on the bus. An argument pursued. The spiky haired boy punched Buddy in the face. Buddy retaliated. He smashed the kid's head against the window, hauled him to the aisle, and gave him a good beating. The kid's friends jumped Buddy from behind. One grabbed him by the neck. Another jabbed Buddy from the side.

Seeing Buddy in trouble, a half dozen of Buddy's boys charged toward the back to join the brawl. Total pandemonium followed. Punches were exchanged. Kicks were thrown. Fists flew in all directions. The bus swirled left and right. It finally stopped by the roadside. The driver called the police and cried for help. Buried beneath a pile of bodies, Buddy struggled to escape. Police sirens neared. The gangs, disentangled, dispersed, unlatched the back emergency exit, and took off running. Buddy and his boys ran, too. When the police arrived, only the girls and nerdy boys remained.

Buddy might have been a rebel on the run, but when it came to Siren, he was the big brother she never had. He was there for her in good times and bad. They studied together, played together, and even worked together. It was Buddy who accompanied Siren to Times Square on frigid winter nights for the annual New Year's Eve ball drop. It was Buddy who landed Siren her first job. On her first day at work in the theater managed by Mr. Schmidt, Buddy tried to show off his popcorn-making skills, but instead, he tripped over a can of oil and spilled it all over the floor.

"Buddy reminds me so much of his dad." Siren laughed. "They both are characters. Mr. Schmidt, besides managing the theater, also manages a piece of property near Brighton Beach. Three summers back he filed a court order to evict one of his tenants who was three months behind in rent. Despite a court order to vacate the property, the tenant refused to budge. Mr. Schmidt took matters into his own hands. He drove to the property in his rundown Volkswagen and tried to enter the house through the back door. The tenant's poodles chased him off."

"That's hilarious," I said, cuddling with Siren in bed. "He sounds like one of my mom's friends."

Chapter 16

MR. SCHMIDT'S
CUBAN CIGAR

S IREN BROUGHT ME to the theater where she had previously worked on a Wednesday evening. Mr. Schmidt was in the awful cigar-smoke-filled projection room putting a reel in place when Siren and I sneaked up on him from behind.

"What're you doing in here?" Siren asked.

"Hi, sweetheart! It's good to see you again." Mr. Schmidt pulled Siren into a bear hug.

"Mr. Schmidt, I want you to meet Victor, a friend from college," Siren said.

"Where are you from, son?"

"Born and raised in North Carolina," I said.

"I took Buddy fly-fishing there when he was five. If my old brain still holds, we caught a bucket full at Little River."

"That's in South Carolina," Siren said.

"By golly, you're right. It is South Carolina." Mr. Schmidt scratched his head.

"Why aren't you downstairs keeping an eye on things?" Siren asked.

"Frankie bailed out on me today," Mr. Schmidt said. "That old dog, he didn't miss a day of work in twenty years, and this morning he had to call in sick."

"No one stays healthy forever."

"Frankie does."

"Shouldn't he be retired?"

"Not without me, he won't. We'll work in this place until we're old and dead."

"I like the new setup downstairs," Siren said.

"Do you? I had the lobby redone two months after you left."

"The parquet is a hundred and ten percent improvement over the moldy carpet we used to have. And I love the way you hang those life-size black-and-white portraits of movie stars from the ceiling."

"What do you think of the *new* pink neon sign above the concession stand?"

"It's eye-catching. But what happened to the ice bin underneath it?"

"I moved it to a separate room to make space for the two new popcorn warmers."

"What about the old crew? Is anyone still around?"

"Everyone except Blondie and Troy. Troy moved to Ohio to live with his girlfriend, and I fired Blondie."

"What did she do this time?"

"A day before an early screening two weeks back, her cash register was short two hundred dollars. She claimed that one of the girls in the afternoon shift pocketed the money. She lied."

"How did you know she wasn't telling the truth?"

"Frankie spotted her slipping some twenties into her purse when he went downstairs to check on the sound in the auditorium."

"Why am I not surprised?" Siren said. "Do you know what I caught her doing last summer?"

"Don't tell me she stole money from your cash register."

"She's too clever for that."

"What did she do, then?"

"She sneaked inside the theater auditorium after the crowd cleared, gathered a couple of empty popcorn buckets from the floor, returned to the concession stand, filled the buckets with fresh popcorn, and sold them to customers."

"I'll be damned. Why didn't you tell me?"

"I couldn't rat on her. If I sold her out, she would know. I was the only one who saw what she did. Knowing her, she would have sabotaged me the next time around for revenge. Besides, I thought she really needed the cash."

"For what?" Mr. Schmidt asked.

"That same day before she sold the popcorn, she seemed upset about something. I asked her what was wrong, and she complained that her mother was having trouble paying some medical bills."

"Was Troy a part of this money-making scheme, too?"

"No way. He's really a nice and honest kid. Don't let his punk rock hairstyle, leather jacket, and nose ring fool you."

"That boy sure can polish those brass door handles."

"But he did a lousy job of controlling the crowd," Siren said. She explained to me what happened one Friday afternoon. An hour before the theater opened, four antsy senior citizens were already in line screaming and hollering. By one o'clock the line stretched around the theater. Troy unlocked the door, and the horde stampeded inside. An old woman and her nine-year-old grandchild rushed into the theater along with the crowd. The woman tripped on the doormat and fell flat on her face. She got right back up and complained. Troy rewarded the old woman with a bag of Skittles and a season pass.

"You kids are something else. I don't know what I would have done without you." Mr. Schmidt reached inside his shirt pocket and removed a handsome silver case. Inside were five bat-size Cuban cigars. "Here, son; try one."

"No, thanks," I said. "I don't smoke."

"Come on, try one," Mr. Schmidt insisted. "It's a gift from me to you. Smoking one of these builds character in a man."

"No, really. I shouldn't."

"Here, take one. Taste the anise and sweet spices. Flavor the cedar and charred nuts. Their woody draw will burn your soul."

I took one to be polite, lit it, sucked a lung full, and choked. Smoke gushed from my mouth and nose like cannon balls. My head swelled, and my eyes reddened. Mr. Schmidt laughed. And Siren laughed.

Chapter *17*

UNINVITED GUEST

S IREN DID NOT EXPECT Mr. Schmidt to last as long as he had in the theater business. Over the years he had lived through a number of robberies. One in particular caught Siren and me off guard. On the Wednesday evening Siren and I visited Mr. Schmidt, shortly after my cigar-smoking experience, a gunman in a sleeveless winter coat sneaked upstairs and hid in the storage closet next to the projection room. Downstairs in the lobby two teenagers ordered a bucket of popcorn and entered the auditorium showing *A League of Their Own*. Behind the concession stand, and beneath a flickering, pink neon sign, Popcorn Candies and Drinks, Mr. Schmidt leafed through a wad of proceeds from the night's sales. Siren and I helped clean the popcorn popper, refilled the ice bin, and locked the candy case. When everything was in order, we followed Mr. Schmidt upstairs. We made our way through the narrow hallway to Mr. Schmidt's office. Mr. Schmidt led the pack. Siren was a step or two behind me.

Our footsteps must have alerted the gunman. The man barged from his hiding place, grabbed Siren by the neck, and plugged a pistol into the back of her head. "The door!" the gunman ordered.

Hand trembling and legs shaking, Mr. Schmidt worked the lock and hurried inside.

The gunman shoved Siren to the floor and ordered me down. He turned the pistol to Mr. Schmidt. "What are you waiting for, fool? Stop shitting in your pants and open the fucking safe. And don't get cute with me!"

Mr. Schmidt spun the combination and removed a thousand dollars from the safe.

Siren cried. The gunman pointed at her. "For Christ's sake, stop crying, Bitch, or I'll blow your fucking brains out!" The gunman swung the pistol back to Mr. Schmidt. "Get down on your fat ass."

Mr. Schmidt followed the gunman's order, and the gunman whacked Mr. Schmidt from behind with the pistol. I was next, and then Siren. All three of us, Mr. Schmidt, Siren, and I, were knocked out cold.

I woke up with a pounding headache. Mr. Schmidt, Siren, and I were strapped in a ball with duct tapes. It took us a good ten minutes to free ourselves. After I called the police, I accompanied Siren and Mr. Schmidt downstairs.

Still shaken from the beating, Mr. Schmidt waddled across the lobby floor. He unlatched the door and walked outside. "Where are the damn cops when we need them?" he blared.

Five minutes later, two police cars swirled to a stop in front of the theater. The officers barged out of their cars with their dogs and flashlights. Mr. Schmidt lit his Cuban cigar. "What took you so long?" he asked. "That son of a bitch is probably in Alaska by now." The cops never caught the gunman.

Chapter 18

LOVE THY HOME FOR
BETTER OR FOR WORSE

T HE THEATER was not a bad place to work. Its flexible hours and entertaining atmosphere kept Siren distracted from the reality of things at home. In contrast to the theater life, things were never okay at home for as long as Siren could remember. For the longest time she felt trapped by Nikolai's control. She wanted out but had nowhere to go. Nikolai was the only family she had. His house was her house. His food was her food, and so she sucked it up and took his abuses.

Mealtimes in particular were dreadful. Siren and Anna often ate in silence. When a conversation did break out, the verbal exchanges were abrupt. Temperamental and emotionally disturbed, Nikolai tolerated no small talk. He was a canister of gas ready to explode. Anything could set him off. If Anna or Siren had something to share, they had to be brief, and the subject discussed had to be important. Otherwise, they were better off keeping their mouths shut. Some men loved small talk, but not Nikolai. Nikolai liked it quiet, so quiet that Siren could hear him chew. The quiet experience at dinner with Nikolai was sickening. The brewing silence chewed at Siren like acids dissolve meat. If disturbed for one reason or another, Nikolai would get up, throw a fist at the table, and bark at Anna, no matter who breached the peace. Anna took the abuse quietly like she did when he forced sex on her early in the morning or late at night, sexual abuses Siren witnessed because Nikolai did not bother to shut his bedroom door.

Siren wanted to give Nikolai a good slap but refrained from doing so, in fear of retaliation. She feared not for her own safety but for Anna's. Anna would suffer the worst consequences; therefore, Siren tried not to set Nikolai aflame.

"You have no idea how fast I swallowed my food, just to get the hell out of his sight," Siren said.

Financial instability had played a major role in shaping Nikolai's hostile behavior and increasingly bad temper. Each day was a struggle. He often worried about not having food to eat. He also feared being ousted from the apartment by the demanding landlord. It was a horrible way to live. He moved from one job to the next and never kept one longer than three months. His jobs varied from working in sweatshops to slaughterhouses, from dishwashing in restaurants to road construction.

Siren felt sorry for him. She felt sorry to see Nikolai returning home dead tired after spending a long night out in subzero winter drilling holes in the street. Each morning, he stripped free of his winter boots, wandered past the living room into the kitchen in his mud-stained pants and sweat-filled shirt, and went through the pots and pans to see what Anna had left him from the night before. Frequently after work, he just slumped into his favorite couch in a corner by the living room window and fell asleep without eating.

"His line of work is a miserable way to make a living," Siren said. "I wish there were better jobs out there for him, but there aren't, not for a man with his education and temperament, anyway."

Financial instability saddened Nikolai. Day in and day out, he kept his frustration pinned inside. "The feeling of inadequacy gnawed at him," Siren said. "Gradually he lost faith in himself, in his family, and in the rest of society. Often he sat alone in the living room dazed in front of the TV or he stood on the back porch, leaning over the metal rail that overlooked the street below." Siren realized what a price Nikolai had paid for freedom. Like countless others who fled their country in search of a better life, he was traumatized by the harsh reality of long work hours and unfulfilled dreams. Like numerous others, Nikolai turned to alcohol to soothe his pain. Whether it was three o'clock in the morning or ten o'clock at night, Nikolai sat by the window and drank. Anna attempted to stop his drinking, but he either responded with rage or simply ignored her. He said she was an old hag who would not leave him alone. "His steadfast alcohol consumption nearly killed him," Siren said. "Following several visits to the Emergency Room for alcohol poisoning, he made an honest attempt to stop. It lasted a month. By Christmas morning, the old habit returned. He gave in to depression and started drinking again."

Liquor was not Nikolai's only addiction. One night when Siren was thirteen, he went into her bedroom and asked her if she could lend him what little money she had saved up from selling lemonade and housekeeping. "We're really strapped for cash this winter," Nikolai said. "Work is not good, and I don't have the heart to tell your aunt that. It's only temporary. I'll pay you back. I promise."

Naive as she was back then, Siren handed Nikolai her savings. He spent every penny of it on cocaine. He even stole seven hundred dollars that Anna stashed away under the kitchen sink. Siren's trust in him went along with the stolen money. It shocked her that a man could do such a thing to his family. She had trusted him, and he had taken advantage of her. Siren felt confused, upset, and betrayed. The thought of her hard-earned money wasted on drugs sickened her.

On numerous nights, Nikolai never made it home. Siren had an idea where he went, thinking he must be at one of his mistresses' place. Anna thought otherwise. Anna told Siren that Nikolai was probably out with his goons getting high on drugs. The food Anna left on the kitchen counter remained untouched. When questioned, he said that he was out working.

"It was all a lie," Siren said. "The expression on his face was a dead giveaway. He kissed up to Anna and pretended to be a good husband whenever he got caught in the act. He even dared to attempt to squeeze more money out of Anna the minute he appeased her. When his effort failed, the friendliness turned into rage."

For the longest time, Siren felt that she was placed on this earth to tolerate Nikolai's erratic and senseless behavior. He instilled in her a sense of hopelessness. Whatever it was, Siren knew that Nikolai had slipped into his own world many years before she set foot into his house. In his sea of solitude he found turbulence instead of peace. His suspicion in life had made him a victim of life. As many victims do, Nikolai had to channel his bitterness and frustration onto someone else. That someone was Anna. She was the one who persistently took his brutal punches. Siren had the unfortunate opportunity to see the abuse unfold before her eyes under the roof of Nikolai's personal torture chamber. When the door opened and friends visited, everything was fine, but when the door was closed, the demon crawled out. No wonder Siren cringed at the thought of returning home. It explained why she had kept her silence for so long. Home was supposed to be a place where she could feel safe. Siren never felt safe with Nikolai in her life and in Anna's life, but for some unexplained reasons Siren felt an obligation to stick with her family no matter how bad things get.

Siren hated the guilt Nikolai instilled in her and Anna for his misery. He wanted them to suffer because he could not get a grip on his own life. Siren had enough problems of her own, and the last thing she needed was to deal with a hopeless drunk and a drug addict who was as stubborn as a mule. Siren knew there was nothing that she or Anna could do or say to change Nikolai, she felt guilty not trying. Her determination to iron out the wrinkles in his life proved fruitless. His psychological mind games, his lies, and his abuse were too much. They wore her out. Subjected to his constant irrational behaviors, abuses, and uncertainty, a part of her died.

Chapter 19

THE NIGHT
NO ANGEL SANG

SIREN'S WORLD turned upside down a night before her sixteenth birthday. It was a cold winter night. An argument broke out between Nikolai and Anna the moment Siren set foot into the house.

"I'll call the police if you continue to hang out with those scumbags!" Anna screamed.

"What are you blabbing about? I was out working last night," Nikolai claimed.

"No, you weren't! Your foreman called. He threatened to fire you if you fail to show up one more night."

"You're lying. I'm busting my ass trying to earn a few dollars so that you and Siren can have a roof over your head, and what do I get in return? I get nothing but false accusations."

"It's the truth, and you know it," Anna said.

"You should be grateful that you have a man like me. Do you see those whores out there in the streets? They're giving blowjobs to strange men for ten bucks a head. That's what you'd be doing without my paychecks."

"What paychecks? The few dollars that you earned, you squandered."

"I'm not going to stand here and put up with this nonsense," Nikolai said. "You're giving me a headache."

"All I'm asking is that you stop doing whatever you're doing," Anna pleaded.

"What am I doing? Please tell me."

"I know things have been hard for all of us, but turning to drugs is not the answer. Can't you see what it's doing to you? Try to be a man, for goodness sake."

Nikolai strayed into the kitchen. Anna followed. Outside, Cimmerian clouds moved aside and unmasked the effulgent moon.

"Aren't you ashamed?" Anna asked. "You lied, stole, and cheated Siren out of her life savings. Look at me when I'm talking to you!"

Nikolai grabbed a beer from the refrigerator and gulped it down.

Anna approached Nikolai and placed her palm on his shoulder. "Please, I beg you," Anna said. "Give up the drugs, and let's try to rebuild our lives."

"Damn it! Can't you see it's too late?" Nikolai smashed the tabletop. Spoons and forks rattled. Barbecue wings flew to the floor.

"It's never too late. Stop acting like a child for once and try to think about your family."

"Don't talk to me about family! I have no family!"

"Whatever happened to the man I fell in love with?" Anna sobbed.

"He died a long time ago. You buried him." Nikolai took out another beer.

"Don't say that!"

"What do you want me to say? That I'm well and happy? Why don't you do me a favor and leave me alone? All I want is some peace and quiet after a long day at work. Is that too much to ask?" Nikolai rubbed his hands over his face.

"I only want the best for you. You know that, don't you?" she pleaded.

"I'm sick and tired of you following me around and ruining my life!"

"Who's ruining whose life?"

"Will you leave me alone? If you want to bitch, go outside and bitch at the dogs!"

Anna exploded. "Is this how you thank me for trying to save your ass?"

Nikolai grabbed Anna by the shoulder and shook her. "What did just you say?"

"Let me go! You're hurting me."

"No, not until you tell me what you just said."

"Let me go, you bastard!" Anna bit Nikolai and yanked herself free.

Stultified, Siren froze in a corner and watched in tears.

"How dare you!" Nikolai screamed. "I want you out of my house tonight. Do you hear me?"

"No! Never! This is my house, too. This is where I belong. If you want to leave, you leave!"

Nikolai slammed a chair to the floor and lunged at Anna. "I'll kill you, ungrateful bitch!"

Anna swung wildly to fend off Nikolai's blows. "Stop it! Stop it!"

Seeing Anna in trouble, Siren shook free her fear and clawed Nikolai from behind. Nikolai swirled back, smashing Siren on the jaw, and sent her crashing into the wall.

"Stay out of this, or I'll beat the living shit out of you!" Nikolai threatened.

Anna, a hundred pounds lighter, grabbed hold of Nikolai again and pounded at him with all she had. Nikolai snatched her by the throat, raised her in the air, and slammed Anna to the floor. "The hell with you!" he cursed, kicking Anna on the chest.

Siren sprang out of the kitchen door and fled downstairs at full speed. "Buddy! Wake up!" she cried, banging on Buddy's window.

The window lit up.

"Siren? What's wrong?" Buddy asked.

"Anna is in trouble! Hurry!"

Wasting no time, Buddy scrambled for his pants and jumped out of the window. Siren started running.

Upstairs in Siren's apartment, Nikolai was gone.

"Where is she?" Buddy asked.

"In there!"

The kitchen was a total wreck. Shattered dishes and glass chips littered the floor. Pots and pans were dented with marks from Nikolai's aluminum bat. Chairs were torn to pieces. The table leaned with only one leg standing. On the floor next to an empty toolbox and a couple of broken knives was Anna. A pool of blood circled the bottom of her head. Wasting no time, Buddy hoisted Anna on his shoulder and fled down the flight of stairs to the parking lot. Siren slipped into the back seat of Buddy's station wagon and helped him shove Anna inside. "This is not happening. This can't be happening to me," Siren said in between sobs.

Buddy fired the engine, placed the gear in reverse, and swirled out of the parking lot. "Everything is going to be all right," he said. "Just take a deep breath and let it go."

The traffic light turned red. Hands shaking, Siren held on to Anna. Buddy rolled down the window to let in some air. The light turned green. He floored the gas pedal and sped down the street. The FM station announced a traffic jam ahead, a fourteen-car pileup. "Jesus Christ," Buddy cursed. "How could this be possible?"

Three policemen at the center of the road redirected the crawling traffic. Buddy stopped the car. The traffic cops continued to push the traffic forward. An ambulance raced by. "How is she holding up?" Buddy inquired.

"She's cold." Siren held onto Anna's hand.

"Hang in there. We're almost there."

An officer finally gave a go signal. Buddy took off and hurried to a nearby hospital.

Four hours later, a nurse in a blue uniform walked into the waiting room and directed Siren and Buddy into the Trauma Unit. Video monitors, IV equipments, and electrodes filled the room. At the center of the cubicle was Anna, a white bandage wrapped over her head and IVs hooked to her arm and legs. A plastic tube ran into her mouth. Wires and electrodes were attached to her chest and strung across the bed like a bulk of tangled telephone wires.

A young nurse in her mid-twenties and an elderly man walked up. The nurse spoke. "This is our head neurologist, Dr. Johnson."

"How's she doing?" Siren asked.

"We're doing everything we can," the neurologist replied.

"Is she going to be all right?"

"We don't know yet. The good news is she suffered no lung, kidney, or intestinal damage. The X-ray showed some fractured bones, but we can fix those."

"What's the bad news?"

"I'm concerned about what is happening inside her head. She took quite a beating."

Siren was aware of that. She was there. She saw the event as it unfolded and felt guilty for not interfering sooner before things spiraled out of control. She saw how Anna clawed at him as she grasped for air. She also saw how Nikolai tossed Anna to the floor like a rag doll. Nikolai had done wrong in the past but he had gone too far this time. No one, especially Anna, should be subject to such abuse. Siren wanted to personally kill him for that. She wanted to avenge Anna for all the years of misery and suffering that Anna had endured. All her life, Anna had been a saint. She wanted to make a difference in people's lives. She wanted to make a difference in her husband's life. She knew Nikolai's weakness and was determined to fill the empty hole. She had given up too much and received too little. Such unselfishness came with a cost. It came with a price that not even all of her lifetime of yard sale proceeds could pay.

"How serious is it?" Siren asked.

"According to the diagnostic imaging report, an area of hemorrhagic contusion was seen in the left frontal region near the mid-line."

"I don't understand."

"Anna is in a coma," the neurologist said. "There's internal bleeding in her head. Both hemispheres of her brain are affected."

"How long will it be before she wakes up?" Buddy asked.

"It's too early to tell. It may take days, weeks, or even months."

"What's the worst scenario?" Buddy asked.

"There's a possibility that she might not wake up. Patients with major head trauma have been known to undergo a persistent vegetative stage."

"No, don't say that!" Siren shook her head. She buried her face on Buddy's chest and broke out in tears.

"Everything is going to be all right," Buddy said. "Everything is going to be all right."

Siren knew that everything was not going to be all right. She knew Buddy had to say what he said because he was all she had. He was like a big brother to her and a big brother needed to do what every big brother does best, protect his sister at all costs, even if it means having to cover up the truth.

The neurologist looked down. "I'm sorry. Only time can tell. I'll run another test in an hour and get a second opinion with other experts. If and when Anna does wake up, she probably won't remember what happened. Right now, you two have to stay strong and be patient. The healing process takes time."

Anna was stabilized. She showed no sign of limb movements at first. She was unable to breathe on her own for a while. An oxygen pump continued to inject air into her lungs. The CAT scan showed that the swelling stopped.

"I felt so helpless," Siren told me. "All I could do was sit and wait."

Each morning before breakfast Siren and Buddy drove to the hospital to check on Anna. When the nurse told them that no visitations were allowed before 11:00 a.m., they stood outside Anna's room and waited until the supervising nurse let them in.

The incident changed Siren's life forever. She could not get over the sight of seeing Anna stretched out on the hospital bed with tubes and wires running all over her body. "Who would have imagined that something like this could happen to someone so close?" Siren asked.

Siren spent New Year's Eve in Anna's hospital room while the rest of the world celebrated. She stood in the dark by the window praying for Anna's recovery. She swore in vain that she would never forgive Nikolai for what he did. She knew he was not a loving husband to Anna, but what he did was unforgivable. "Stay strong," Siren recalled her pastor's words. "God always opens new doors where others have recently been shut. Something positive will come out of this." In the dark, still as a rock, Siren stood and looked out the window. Her eyes reddened from lack of sleep. The melancholy atmosphere reminded Siren of how fragile life could be.

Out in the hallway, the sound of footsteps accompanied the low droning of the air vent. "Susan, call the doctor!" a female voice shrieked. "She's not breathing!" another responded.

The death cry, the long hours ahead, and Siren's already burdening work schedule did not offer any reprieve for her troubled mind. "What the hell is wrong with you, God?" Siren asked. "You don't give a damn, do you?" In Siren's mind, her God must answer. Nothing else mattered, and nothing else was acceptable. Her God did not answer, though, and so she stood in silence and fumed. The clock on the wall ticked. The fireworks continued to twinkle from the TV screen. This luminescence embraced Anna's bed and plastered the get-well cards and flower vase on the window ledge.

Anna was hospitalized for months before she could return home. Whatever happened between Nikolai and

Anna following her release from the hospital, Siren did not say. Nikolai was not charged with assault because no charges were filed against him. From what I gathered after talking to Joe, the old man next door, the whole thing was a big accident, an accident that the police found hard to believe.

Joe also said that Anna ran out of her apartment one night and killed herself. Joe was there that night. He was sitting on the front porch at his usual spot like he did when Siren and I arrived. He saw it all. He saw how Anna ran out of the apartment and dived headfirst down the concrete stairs. Siren and Nikolai raced out of the apartment too, but they were too late. Anna's head smashed onto the concrete, and her skull cracked. She died instantly. Her body spread motionless on the stairs like a frozen white butterfly.

Joe, Mr. and Mrs. Schmidt, Buddy, and even Nikolai accompanied Siren to the wake. Siren wore a black dress. Nikolai had on a matching black outfit. Buddy wore a lavender tie. "It was quite a sight to walk into a roomful of unfamiliar grievers," Joe said. "I didn't know that Anna had so many friends. Blacks, Asians, Hispanics, Russians, and the whole spectrum of races packed the room. Even those neighborhood women who jeered Anna because of her parsimonious activities showed up to pay their respects. They all gathered to mourn the death of a saint."

Anna was nicely dressed. Her hair was elegantly combed. She lay peacefully inside the cedar coffin with her head resting on a pillow. Red, white, and pink flowers surrounded Anna. Nikolai melted as he approached her. Joe watched Nikolai cry. Knees on the floor and hands on the coffin, Nikolai cried. "No! No! No! You can't leave me like this! This is not right! This is not how things are supposed to end. I'm sorry! I'm sorry! Please forgive me!"

Siren, Joe, Buddy, and Mr. and Mrs. Schmidt escorted Nikolai outside. They stood in the hall until he calmed.

Chapter 20

IOTA

O UR STAY IN NEW YORK CITY WAS
SHORT. Siren and I spent a part of our first-
full day in the Big Apple doing household
chores. We washed the dishes, took out the trash, vacu-
umed the floor, and rid Nikolai's apartment of its terrible
smell while Nikolai sat on the couch in his usual spot,
dazed in front of the flickering TV. When the kitchen
sink was polished and the bathroom floor was scrubbed,
we worked on Siren's room. Compared to the rest of the
apartment, cleaning her room was not as big a challenge.
It was a small room with a bed, a mirror, a dresser, a desk,
and four shelves full of books. Siren was a voracious
reader. She had them all: Bunin, Brodsky, Eliot, Hem-
mingway, Rolland, and Fitzgerald.

Siren took me out to explore the city after we finished the household chores. We went to Central Park, Chinatown, Fifth Avenue, and more. At night, we took the Staten Island ferry across the Hudson and watched the Statue of Liberty and the stars from afar. After a long day, we returned to her old room under Nikolai's roof and snuggled in bed with Chucky, a teddy bear Siren had owned since she was six. It was Chucky who gave her comfort when she was young.

Few words were exchanged between Nikolai and Siren during our stay, and no words were exchanged between Siren and him as we departed. Two days after our arrival in Brooklyn, Siren and I left to return to North Carolina. Nikolai stood on the front porch and watched us leave. There was a light sprinkle that day. He looked sad. Siren also looked sad. She probably forgave him for what he had done to Anna, but she certainly did not forget. I saw it in her eyes, those piecing eyes. She appeared more traumatized by her past than by the hostage situation that we faced at Mr. Schmidt's theater from the night before.

Part IV

A TIME TO SEW

Stillwater 1992

Chapter 21

PORT OF HEAVEN

OLIVER WENDELL HOLMES ONCE
WROTE that to "reach the port of heaven, we
must sail sometimes with the wind and some-
times against it, but we must sail, and not drift, nor lie at
anchor." Siren and I did just that. We sailed, sometimes
with the wind and sometimes against the wind, but we
sailed. The time was the summer of 1992, a summer to be
remembered in the short chapter of our life together. On
a hot day with some breaking clouds, Siren and I left
Chapel Hill, North Carolina. It was a perfect day for driving. Trailing behind a half dozen other cars, we snaked
our way across the narrow and rugged Appalachian
Mountain path. At the time, I thought Siren's archaic
four-cylinder hatchback would never make it to the top.
Her brakes were bad, and the loads were heavy. Pixie

choked in the extreme heat as she slowly made her way up the ravine. I kept my fingers crossed, hoping an oncoming car would not swerve out of control and knock Pixie off the cliff. Siren and I would have plunged into the heart of the ravine. Fortunately, we drove, and drove and all was fine.

It took us a good day drive to reach Nashville, Tennessee. After a quick night out in town listening to musicians playing bluegrass and old-time tunes, Siren and I prepared for our weeklong training. We got up at six o'clock, took a cold shower, and went off to our daily drills. In the morning we attended sales classes to learn the tricks of the trade. In the afternoon, we teamed up with field experts to perfect our sales pitch and people approaching skills. At the close of the day, we returned to our hotel room and prepared materials for the next day's run. Once we mastered the ins and outs of the business, we said farewell to Music City USA.

For the first time in our lives, our guts wrenched with excitement and fear. Like other college students joining the sales program, Siren and I had no idea what we were getting ourselves into. Some of us were assigned to cover the Great Lakes region. Others were shipped out west to California. The rest had to go as far north as Fargo, North Dakota. Wherever our destinations, we all knew that we were up for an adventure of a lifetime.

I was a skeptic when Siren first told me about Hellas Books, so I made some inquiries to find out more about the company I was about to join.

"It's a fraud," a friend from a nearby university warned. "The company promises money and opportunities. They lure college kids from across the country to join their program, but many of those who sign up and go through the process are extremely disappointed. One guy I knew made a hundred bucks the whole summer."

"Give me a break," I said. "Even a five-year-old could make more than that selling lemonade. The guy probably sat on his dumb ass all summer long doing nothing when he should have been running the street in his ten-dollar sneakers, wheeling and dealing and knocking on doors."

I refused to believe that anyone with a will to work could come up with only a hundred dollars for two months' worth of work. Then again, what did I know? I never had to break a sweat in my life, let alone try to make it on my own several thousands miles away from home. It was one thing to talk the talk, but another to walk the walk. Before I walked the walk, I first had to sell my plan to my father.

"Are you out of your mind?" he reacted. "Who's going to buy books from you? You're not a salesman."

My father was right. I was no salesman. I knew that, and he knew that, but I planned to be one, at least for a summer.

"Do you know what you're getting yourself into? There are crazy people out there."

Again, my father was right. Behind every closed door, a potential killer lurked. I could be mugged, beaten, or even shot. The thought of venturing into unknown territory did terrify me; however, the alternative, spending the summer worrying about Siren, scared me even more.

"If it's my time to go, I can die crossing a street," I said.

"But why expose yourself to unnecessary risks, Son?"

"I want to do something different," I said. "I want to see what's out there. What's the point of wasting away the summer in D.C. catering to the trivial needs of some U.S. senator? Besides, I could use some fresh air and open country." Those were my words, and that was that. My mind was set. Not even my father could talk me out of it. I stuck with my gut and ran head on with fate. It felt right, a visceral feeling only the subconscious mind could explain. In the end, my father yielded. He respected my decision and let me go. He decided to let me get a taste of life and allow reality do the slapping.

Siren was not too crazy, either, about joining the Hellas Books sales force, but she had no choice. She could suck it up and take the job or spend another summer in her hometown working in Mr. Schmidt's theater or flipping burgers for $4.50 an hour at Jacky Jones Burgers & Grill. The choice was hers. She needed the money, and the only way to make the type of money she needed was through door-to-door sales. It might be hard work, but the money was good, and it was legitimate. She knew the perils involved and was prepared to face them all.

Despite her potential psychological or physical obstacles, there was little doubt in my mind that Siren would succeed. It was within her nature to succeed. She was the real reason I signed up for the door-to-door sales. I did not join Hellas Books sales team for the money. I had three million in my bank account from stocks earnings alone. Who in his right mind would join a company for the fresh air, knowing the hard work ahead? There were other ways of getting fresh air. There was plenty of fresh air in the private golf course of my father's country club. I was, after all, the son of a four-star general. The son of a four-star general had many perks. I was not about to give up my comfort to gain discipline, learn the meaning of life, or even catch a breath of fresh country air. I joined Hellas Books because of love, or the thought of love. I wanted to be by Siren's side to provide moral support. I wanted to make sure I was there for my woman when she needed me most. It was a dangerous world out there. I could not bear the thought of seeing her walking the street at night alone. A stranger could snatch her from behind and have a good time with her. She could be killed. Like my father said, anything goes in this crazy world. Despite my good intentions, I dared not tell Siren my true motive. She would have been flabbergasted. I knew I was being chivalrous, but to allow her to expose to the dangers alone was unacceptable. To be on equal footing, I did something I would have never done had it been for anyone else. I agreed to forego all the conveniences of life to be with her.

"If a mother of five can raise a family single-handedly, you can survive a couple of months without your fancy Rolex watch and your expensive car," Siren said.

I abided by Siren's rule and reluctantly left everything behind, including my banking cards, cell phone, and my Mercedes convertible. It was hard to stash away my safety net, but I did it. Not even my father realized the extent of my sacrifice. Siren was surprised and impressed that I would go out of my way to perform such an honorable act. I later learned that it was an act not for her benefit, but for mine.

With less than two hundred dollars between the two of us, Siren and I crossed the Tennessee border and made our way north to the heartland of America. We ventured into the flat plains of Kentucky and cut through the cow fields of Indiana. We drove onward, sometimes half asleep and sometimes fully awake. Our thirst for adventure pushed us on. However we drove and whatever roads and avenues we took, we were never bored. In every new mile of pastureland and every new town and city, a treasure trove awaited us. We drove through lush grass fields dotted with farmhouses, straw barns, gristmills, old warehouses, and creeping kudzu. We drove through ramshackle roadside where wide-eyed kids played in dirty brown clothes. For the first time in my life, I laid aside my misconceptions of what America truly holds.

At Remington, Indiana, the sun was already on its way down. Its large red ring slowly sank below the horizon. We pulled over and booked a room in a family-owned motel in the middle of nowhere. The only things in sight for miles were the blinking stars and cow pastures with countless spooling haystacks. It was a clear night. Standing on the upper deck, Siren and I watched the grazing land and its vanilla-colored surface nestled like a dune of sand. It would have been a beautiful sight to enjoy, had it not been for the putrid stench of dung heaps that quickly drove us inside. The following morning, we grabbed two king-size chocolate-covered donuts from the reception lodge and went on our way. Around noon, we stopped at Wendy's and had three-quarter pound burgers, big square burgers with lettuce, tomato, and onion. They were the best burgers I ever had. The long road trip must have brought out the appetite in me. Maybe the burger up North simply tasted better than those from down South. Whatever the reasons, Siren and I ventured onward with a fuller stomach.

Chapter 22

LOOKING AT SAINT CROIX

I T TOOK US A GOOD THREE-THOUSAND-
MILE drive to reach Stillwater, Minnesota. Stillwater was a picturesque town twenty miles east of
downtown St. Paul. With a population less than twenty
thousand, the family-oriented community nuzzled into
the bluffs of the St. Croix River. A town of scenic waterways sitting in the wooded hills of the St. Croix Valley,
Stillwater held a turn-of-the-century charm. Multicolored lights reflected in its river. Pin-size glitters of the
town could be seen miles away on clear summer nights.
Shops, taverns, and restaurants lined Main Street, a street
once occupied by rooming houses, saloons, theaters,
breweries, and railroad buildings.

The Lakota and Ojibwa tribes once lived on this land.
Back in the eighteenth and nineteenth century, these

American Indian tribes relied on the river as a source of food and transportation. Then came the fur traders and the lumber barons who utilized the waterways for transporting pelts and logs.

Up into the late 1800s, Stillwater was a thriving logging town. At the heart of Stillwater was its historic downtown district, the birthplace of Minnesota. It was a place where outlaws were once imprisoned and fortunes were once made in lumber and milling. No longer a logging town, antique stores and retail shops filled the streets.

Siren and I arrived in Stillwater late on a misty afternoon in a light drizzle. Men in black tuxedos and women in white dresses hurried out of limousines that lined the street. They fled toward a large paddle-wheel boat docked by the water's edge. On the upper level of the swan-like boat men and women danced to the tune of a jazz band. Others gathered in the promenade deck for the river view.

"We're here at last!" Siren said, wasting no time unclamping her seatbelt and hurrying out of the car.

I removed the key from the ignition and joined her outside. With an umbrella over our heads we embraced and watched the falling rain. Excitement filled the air. Along with the excitement came fear. The newness, unfamiliarity, and potential hostility concerned us.

"I wonder how the people in this small town are going to treat us," Siren said.

"I don't know, but we're about to find out," I responded, rushing Siren along to Big Joe, a small diner by the water. At the foot of the diner door, a crippled vagabond greeted us with a song. "Velvet rain, velvet rain, come pour on me velvet rain," he sang. I tossed two quarters into his cutout sardine can and stepped inside. All activities stopped. There was nothing but silence. Dead silence. It was as silent as the black and white photos of the sport legends on the wall. I heard a spoon drop. All eyes were on Siren and me, two strangers in a town where everyone knew everyone else.

"I don't think we're welcome here," Siren said in a hushed tone. She guardedly studied the crowd.

"Don't worry," I said. "They'll love us. Just act nice and smile."

The patrons, waiters, waitresses, cashier, and even the two police officers sitting near the door stared us down. They studied us, and we studied them. It was amusing to be caught in this most pronounced visual modality. Our childlike curiosity toward each other would have made world-famous child psychologist Jean Piaget proud.

Given the unknown terrain, I instinctively stood still. So did Siren.

"If you don't know your adversaries' motive, be patient, watch, and wait," my father had taught me. "Be on your guard and wait. If you wait long enough they'll make the first move. It is then that you can decide to attack, defend, or retreat." Yielding to those stone-carved words, I held Siren's hand and waited. The crowd's gazes disengaged. They realized we were not a threat. Normalcy resumed. The racket started again and conversations once more filled the room.

"Good evening. My name is Marie-Anne. I'll be your waitress tonight." A waitress in red-apron greeted us.

Siren stopped the waitress before she turned and led the way. "Is there a phone in here that we can use to make a quick call?"

Marie-Anne turned, faced the crowd, and pointed to a narrow hallway behind the last table in the rear. "There's a pay phone next to the men's room in the back," she said.

Siren and I thanked Marie-Anne and sped through the crowd. Although most had lost interest in us, some still had not. Their gaze followed us until we turned the corner.

In the dingy confine of a narrow hallway, a dim fluorescent bulb flickered overhead. A black and silver phone hung low against the log-lined wall. Siren dug inside her purse and removed her pocketsize phone book. In it was a number for Nadia, Nikolai's aunt, whom he had not seen in years. Siren did not know much about Nadia except that she lived in Stillwater. She found out the night before our departure from Nashville, when she phoned home to inform Nikolai of our destination. All those years, Nikolai had kept the great secret from Siren, the secret of the name and whereabouts of his estranged wealthy aunt Nadia, younger sister of his deceased mother, Nina. Whatever the reason may be, whether out of shame, regret, or dark family secrets, Nikolai had not been in touch with Nadia for a long time. The only reason he had called her, I presumed, was out of obligation not to Nadia but to Siren. He owed it to Siren for all that she had done and for all that she had endured. Considering the pain he had put Siren through, it was the least he could do to redeem himself. Besides, Nadia needed the company, and Siren and I needed a place to stay. It was a perfect setup.

Siren slipped a quarter into the coin slot, dialed Nadia's number, and waited. The phone rang.

"Hello?" a grandmotherly voice uttered, just loud enough for me to hear with my ear pressing near.

"Is this Nadia?" Siren asked.

"This is she."

"Hi, Nadia! This is Siren," she spit out excitedly.

"Where are you, dear?"

"I'm inside Big Joe. I just arrived in Stillwater."

"It would be nice if she can meet us here," I whispered into Siren's ear. We had endured a long trip, and the last thing we needed was to get lost in the rain in an unfamiliar town when the light had already begun to fade.

"Stay where you are, dear," Nadia instructed. "I will be there in five minutes."

I sighed in relief.

Chapter 23

PINK CADILLAC

O UTSIDE BIG JOE, under a green awning, the beggar continued to sing. "Velvet rain, velvet rain, come pour on me velvet rain." The drizzle had thinned out into an oily gray haze. Before long, a pink Cadillac showed up and crawled to a stop an inch from the curve. A petite elderly woman with bushy white hair waved at us from behind a large steering wheel. In the back seat a small puppy, white with reddish-brown spots, jumped up and down and barked. Seeing Siren and me approaching, the creature leaped from the back seat and landed on Nadia's lap.

"It's so nice to finally meet you!" Siren exclaimed. She leaned in the driver's window and pecked Nadia on the cheek.

"You are such a lovely young lady," Nadia said. "Niko-lai never mentioned how beautiful you are."

Flustered by the unexpected compliment, Siren turned her attention to the dog. "Hi, cutie!" The creature's jet black eyes lit up. It wagged its tail. Siren reached for the dog on Nadia's lap and brought him outside.

"Oh dear, Storm likes you," Nadia said.

"I think we're going to get along fine." Siren combed the creature's well-groomed fur with her fingers. Even his paws were spotlessly clean. "I have never seen anything like him. What breed is he?"

"Storm is a Brittany Spaniel, and he loves to stalk squirrels."

"How old is he?"

"He is a year old. A year and two months, to be exact."

Only fourteen months old, and Storm acted like he was the king of the world. A preening peacock of a dog, he was self-absorbed, egotistic, and stubborn on the verge of haughtiness. He aspired to be a hero of all dogs. He lambasted me with his pompous barks and acted as though destined for greatness and immortality. However pretentious Storm might have appeared, he was entertaining. He was also Nadia's most loyal companion.

"You like listening to us, don't you?" Siren cooed. Storm barked and wiggled his tail. He cuddled comfortably in Siren's arm and acted like he understood what was said, as if he wanted to voice his opinion too, but all he could do was bark. He barked at Siren, and he barked at me.

"And who might this handsome young man be?" Nadia asked.

I stepped closer to the car and introduced myself. "I'm Victor," I said.

"I know who you are, silly!" Nadia grinned. "I am just teasing. Nikolai told me all about you."

"Really?"

"You don't think I would let a stranger into my house without first doing a little checking, do you?"

"I hope it's nothing bad," I said. Nikolai and I did not exactly get along during my brief visit to New York. In fact, we barely spoke.

"Don't worry, dear. It is all good." Nadia spelled out my credentials. "Brilliant and handsome, a trait I always look for in a man," she closed.

Shocked, I allowed the news to sink in. I had never expected Siren to brag about me. How did she know I was the president of the National Honor Society or the captain of my high school varsity soccer team? Who told her I had a perfect score on the SAT or won the National Merit scholarship? There was only one logical explanation. It had to be my friends. Knowing Siren, she probably worked her charm on them, like women do when they need to extract information from men. My friends, typical men they were—young, restless, and hormone driven—would spill their heart out for a girl like Siren. All she needed to do was throw a smile and walk an inch closer to impose her womanly presence on them. Whatever information she heard about me, Siren did an amazing job of keeping her acquired knowledge a secret. What threw me off was her confiding my background to Niko-lai. Why would she do such a thing? I thought she hated him. If she found him so repugnant, why would she want to tell him about me? How significant was I to him? Was I the bargaining tool in the family negotiation table? Was I the neutral factor that served to bridge their tattered relationship?

For a moment, I felt like a prized possession at an auc-tion. What befuddled me most was that Nikolai actually remembered the details about me and managed to pass them along to someone I had never anticipated meeting. I thought he could not care less, even if I was Ivan the Great. A drunk, a drug addict, and a wife abuser, I never pictured him as a concerned uncle who took great pride in his niece's boyfriend. The whole thing seemed rather odd. Maybe Siren was closer to Nikolai than I thought. Regardless, the word had spread and it caught the atten-tion of an old woman in a place several thousand miles from home.

"How was the drive up here?" Nadia inquired.

"It was not so bad," I said.

"Victor took a wrong turn in Kentucky," Siren added, "and we ended in downtown Louisville."

"Oh, dear. Did you have any problem finding your way back onto the highway?"

"Nope. Siren is an excellent navigational partner. I can always depend on her to guide me out of troubled areas,"

I said. "Come to think of it, I'm glad we made the wrong turn. Scenic routes are the best way to travel."

"Only if you're young and have all the time in the world," Siren added.

"Someone must have not kept an eye on the road," Nadia said.

"It's all Victor's fault," Siren said.

"I was sleepy, okay?"

"You shouldn't be behind the wheel, then," Nadia warned. She inched closer to the car window and looked me in the eyes.

"I told him it's dangerous, but he insisted on driving. This guy can be quite stubborn sometimes," Siren said.

"You should learn to listen to a woman," Nadia said, looking at me. "She knows what is best."

Siren grinned, nodding.

"One of my friends suffered a near fatal accident," Nadia said. "She was young like you and thought she would be fine if she drank coffee to keep awake."

"I bet that didn't last long," I added.

"No, it did not. When the caffeine failed, she turned on the radio."

"I've tried that," I said.

"She even opened the window to let in the air. It was early January. The subzero winter wind was too much for her, so she rolled it back up. 'If I can only make it to the next exit,' she told herself. And in a split second her mind shut down. The next thing she knew, she was mummified on a hospital bed six hundred miles away from home. She had countless stitches on her face, a broken arm, several broken ribs, and a collapsed lung."

"That's horrible! Did she crash into another car?" Siren asked.

"No, worse. She drove into a tree," Nadia said.

"Is she all right now?"

"She is dead."

"From the accident?" I asked.

"Cancer took her life a few years back, but the lesson is most accidents occur when the driver is not fully alert. If you must, have someone else take over the wheel or pull to the side of the road for a quick nap. I know what it is like to be your age. I used to think I was invincible. Safety was not always a priority."

I held Siren up close. "I'll keep that in mind."

Storm growled.

Nadia laughed. "Oh, dear. Stormy is getting jealous."

"Don't worry, Cutie. He won't steal me away from you." Siren rubbed the dog's head. Storm seemed pleased. He closed his eyes and rested his jaw on Siren's arm.

"I used to love long road trips," Nadia said. "But at my age, I cannot do it anymore." Nadia looked at her watch. "We should get going. I don't want you to catch a cold standing out here in this kind of weather."

Siren and I followed Nadia home. Storm joined us for the ride. He snuggled on Siren's lap while I drove.

It was a short drive to Nadia's place. She lived about a quarter of a mile from the water in an old house surrounded by a small forest of trees. I had no problem following her home. Trailing behind her Cadillac at fifteen miles an hour there was no way in hell I could have gotten lost, even if I tried. There were no other cars on the road so Nadia took her time. Cautious and blind as a bat, she inched her way home. If I had been in a hurry, her tortoise crawl uphill would have driven me mad, but I was in no hurry. Our trip was near an end, and I did not mind the view. It was nice to watch the trees at night after it rained. They hid behind the fog like giant nocturnal creatures with many arms. At the turn of the road, Nadia's Cadillac veered right and made its way to the main entrance of her estate creeping at a snail's pace past an iron gate flanked on both sides by droopy trees.

"Time knows no mercy," Siren said, studying the gate that flapped on its hinges like a giant bird wing. "Whether manmade objects or creatures of godly creation, all things must perish in the end."

Straight ahead, an antiquated Victorian house jutted from the ground. It was no ordinary house. Ivy wrapped all parts of its structure except the windows and door. At night, the grandiose structure glowed like a Halloween pumpkin in the wood. Light from the windows looked like a pair of glowing eyes. In the front yard beneath the trees, a small patch of land laid untended. A one-time tomato garden was filled with weeds and thorns. Footlong herbaceous plants surrounded its perimeter. Their stems spurted from the ground and covered everything in sight except a run-down Renault and a cobblestone trail that pointed toward the front door of Nadia's house.

More surprises awaited Siren and me when Nadia stirred clear the door. The dilapidated structure had Siren and me fooled. It was no rustic bungalow on a windswept beach. Despite its deceptive outer appearance, hidden treasures stretched lavishly inside. Silk robes, intricate jade jewelry, and china filled glass cabinets.

Nadia led Siren and me into the dining room. It became clear that Nadia had taken great care in preparation for our arrival. A mahogany refectory table of intricate filigreed carvings with a banquet-scale dinner awaited Siren and me at the center of the room. On the table was a classic candelabra; silver-plated dome; and holiday dinner wares that included hand-painted serving bowls, serving platters, dinner plates, salad plates, bread and butter plates, and cups and saucers. Such an arrangement honored a special occasion for special guests.

Nadia, Siren, and I sat on the mahogany chairs with multicolored tapestry coat of arms upholstery and held hands for a brief prayer.

"Thank you, Lord, for bringing Siren and Victor safely in their journey to this house," Nadia began. "And thank you, Lord, for blessing us with the food on this table."

It was Siren's turn. "Our Father, we're blessed with Nadia's hospitality and this bountiful meal that she has prepared for us tonight."

Not much of a prayer or a believer, I closed with one word. "Amen."

"Don't be shy. Help yourself," Nadia said. "There's plenty of food to go around." She grabbed a knife and went to work on the hickory-smoked turkey. It was quite a turkey, thrice the size of a hen.

Siren passed the potato and the corn.

"It looks like you have outdone yourself," Siren praised. "The food looks and smells so good."

"There's nothing better than a home-cooked meal," I said.

Nadia threw an appreciative smile. "Cooking keeps me busy." She filled her crystal faceted glass with tea. "It keeps my mind off of things."

"Siren and I are grateful to you for allowing us to stay here for the summer," I said.

"The honor is all mine." Nadia laid a napkin on her lap. "I needed young people like you around. I needed to hear footsteps other than mine. It can get quite lonely living in this big house by myself. At night, there is nothing but the walls, the mirrors, and the doors."

We learned it had been years since Nadia had guests over. After George, her husband, passed away, they all slowly vanished from her life. George was born in another small town in Michigan forty miles north of Detroit. He was second in a family of five siblings. According to Nadia, George was tall, strikingly handsome, and politically savvy. He was a paragon of corporate leadership, a distinguished intellectual, and a caring husband. "There was something about George that drew people to him," Nadia said. "It must have been his acute awareness of all things."

I passed Nadia the gravy bowl. She scooped a spoonful and poured it on the mashed potatoes.

"There is one thing I really miss about George," Nadia continued. "He was such a sweet talker. He used to say, 'Cat Woman, you make the best gravy in town.' Women like that. We liked to be pampered and complimented on the little things in life. And I was no exception."

"Why did he call you Cat Woman?" Siren asked.

"We used to have a black kitten that trailed me around the house. Ketchup, as George called her, followed me upstairs, downstairs, to the attic, to the basement, and even into the bathroom. She would sit on the tile floor next to bathtub and wait patiently while I enjoyed my bubble bath. George found Ketchup amusing. He said she confused me for her mother."

"That's adorable," Siren said.

"Why did George call the cat Ketchup?" I asked.

"Ketchup loved to lick ketchup. One time during dinner, I accidentally dropped a French fry. Did you know what Ketchup did?"

"What?" Siren asked.

"She licked the ketchup clean and left the fry untouched."

"That's funny."

"Ketchup was one odd kitten," Nadia said. "She was as odd as Cotton Ball."

"Who or what is Cotton Ball?"

"Cotton Ball is my bunny," Nadia said. "He *was* my bunny," she corrected herself.

"What made Cotton Ball so odd? Did he like ketchup, too?" I joked.

"No, dear. Cotton Ball liked everything except ketchup and carrot. It was a good thing because he and Ketchup wouldn't have gotten along so well if they'd had to fight for ketchup."

"What did Cotton Ball eat if he did not like carrot and ketchup?" I asked.

"Cotton Ball loved grass, hamburger buns and candy."

"Candy and hamburger buns? That's crazy!"

Nadia smiled. "That is why he got so fat. Do you know how big he got?"

"I'm afraid to ask," I said.

"He was nearly two feet long."

"That's a monster rabbit," Siren said. "I don't think I have seen any rabbit that size in my life."

"Cotton Ball was as big as Storm, if not bigger."

"Are you sure you didn't mistake him for the dog?" I asked.

"Cotton Ball was no dog, not with those big ears. Do you know what he used to do? He used to hop around the house looking for candy while Ketchup chased Buzz."

"Who's Buzz?" I asked.

"Buzz is a dragonfly."

"Buzz, the dragonfly? That's too funny!" Siren laughed.

"Isn't it charming?" Nadia asked. "George named it Buzz because it buzzed before his eyes."

"How did George keep Buzz in the house?" Siren asked.

"He tied one end of a string to Buzz's tail and tied the other end to Ketchup's collar."

"That's mean," Siren said.

"George did not seem to think so. He thought it was funny. I do not know how it worked or who moved first, but Buzz and Ketchup seemed to have a ball together."

"What about Cotton Ball? I thought she and Ketchup played together, too," Siren said.

"Most of the time, when he was not busy searching for candy. George and I used to play a little game with Cotton Ball. We hid lollipops around the house and bet on how long it would take before Cotton Ball located them all."

"Did he?"

"He sure did. He even sneaked under my bed in his hunt."

I looked around. There was no picture of a cat, a rabbit, or a dragonfly.

"What happened to Ketchup and Cotton Ball?" I asked.

Nadia adjusted her grandmotherly spectacles and leaned far forward to impart her dark secret. "There was an accident," she whispered. "They both drowned playing in the bathtub. I left the water running and went downstairs to get a drink. When I came back, Cotton Ball and Ketchup were floating lifeless in the water. Buzz was wet but alive. George let him go." That was that. Nadia went no further. An awkward silence followed.

"Where did you say that you met George?" I asked.

Nadia removed her apron and straightened her back. The melancholy demeanor vanished, and her face beamed.

"George and I met in Kiev," she said.

Kiev, a city of dreams and the cradle of Russian civilization, was a city Siren and I had longed to visit together. Siren had spoken about the city's majestic temples, and its breathtaking domed cathedrals, timeless refectory, and eternally still bell tower. She had also told me about a great aunt who was born and raised in that city, but she did not know until then that this great aunt was Nadia. Fate had an odd way of unfolding events and bringing people together.

Nadia sipped her tea and swallowed with a light gurgle. "Of all the people, it had to be the son of an American diplomat," she proceeded. "Do you see that cup in there?" Her crooked finger trailed to a porcelain teacup inside a swarthy china cabinet a body length to my left. "There is a story behind that cup." She took another sip and cleared her throat. "It all began on an autumn day in 1928, one year after Stalin took power and turned the Ukraine into his personal laboratory for testing Soviet restructuring. George, fresh out of Princeton, decided to take some time off to travel abroad."

"Of all the places in the world, why did he choose the Ukraine?" Siren asked.

"The social and political changes taking place at the time intrigued him," Nadia said. "A change that later resulted in the destruction of countless Ukrainian cathedrals, political executions of intellectuals who were considered dangerous to Stalin's nationalist view, and the starvation of millions in labor camps." A sullen gloom fell over Nadia's face. Suppressed memories of her past sprung back to life. "My parents died in the labor camp," she sadly voiced.

"I'm sorry," I said.

Nadia sipped her tea.

"Where in Kiev did you meet George?" Siren asked.

"I ran into him in one of Kiev's oldest streets in an ancient part of town near St. Andrew's Cathedral. Being the only foreigner in the area, George did his best to conceal himself."

"What do you mean conceal himself? Was he a spy?" I asked.

"Dear, no." Nadia laughed. "George couldn't have been a spy if he wanted to. He was too young and innocent."

"Then why did he want to conceal himself?"

"He didn't like drawing unnecessary attention to himself. Instead of wearing his American clothes he had on a traditional Ukrainian street outfit. He managed to escape the eyes of most locals except mine."

"How did you spot him?" Siren asked.

"I was walking down the street when I heard a child's cry from behind. I turned around and saw George, a nice-looking young man standing on the steep winding stone street. He stood speechless when he saw me looking at him."

"What did you do next?"

"I took a risk and let the stranger approach me. George walked up, introduced himself, and told me how beautiful I looked. He also told me he had been following me. I appreciated that, an honest stalker. My heart skipped when he talked. I was sixteen and had never met an American before. Better yet, he was a handsome young American who spoke perfect Ukrainian. Learning that George had a fascination with my culture, I invited him over to my house for a cup of tea."

"That was very brave of you, to bring a total stranger to your home when you first met him," I said.

"I wanted George to see firsthand the daily life of a Ukrainian family. More importantly, I wanted him to meet my parents. George accepted the offer. My initiative took George by surprise. It also took me by surprise. Words spurted out of my mouth before I even had time to think things through."

"But it worked out well," Siren said.

"It did. My parents loved George. One, he was the son of a diplomat. Two, he held a commanding knowledge of our history. George impressed my father with his knowledge of the tsarist regime and its collapse. He talked about the Mongol invasions in the thirteenth century and about the East Slavic tribes that gave rise to the Russians, Belorussians, and Ukrainians. He also talked about the seventeenth-century Ukrainian Cossacks whose leaders swore allegiance to the Muscovite tsar in exchange for autonomy."

"That's impressive."

"It is. No boy that father knew had such vast knowledge on Ukraine's past. A strong nationalist, father had great respect for any young man with the intellectual appetite for Ukrainian history and politics." Nadia slowed to catch her breath. She took another sip of tea and continued. "My parents were big believers in a good upbringing. They wanted me to meet someone with a good head on his shoulders."

"Was your father concerned at all that George was an American?" I asked.

"No, it did not matter what nationality George was, as long as he could speak our native tongue and understand our way of life. George was bright, ambitious, charming, polite, and responsible. Those qualities instantly won my parents' approval. When he entered my house, my parents invited him into the living room. I asked him if he liked tea or coffee. George said that he preferred tea. I was glad, because we had homegrown tea. While George continued to impress my father with his wealth of knowledge, I went into the kitchen to make George a cup of tea. It was not any regular cup of tea. I made him rose tea. I handpicked the rose petals from our garden in the back of our house. George loved it."

"So that cup of tea marked the start of your relationship with George?" Siren asked.

"Yes. It symbolized the beginning of our lifelong love affair." Glassy eyed, Nadia pinned her hair back. Her gaze remained fixed on the china cabinet. In lighthearted tears and reflective demeanor, she relived the years of her youth. "After dating me for only a few months, George had to leave the Ukraine."

"Why?" Siren asked.

"The changing political scene concerned George's parents. They wanted him out of the country, but George and I were madly in love. He refused to leave the country without me. One evening during dinner, George got on his knee and proposed. The news took my father by surprise."

"Your parents must have been wretched over your departure from Ukraine," Siren said.

"When I was a child, my father had told me that some-day I would be swept off my feet by a prince from some foreign land. On the night of George's proposal, he knew the opportunity had unveiled itself. He also knew his lit-tle girl had grown up and that he had to let her go."

"What about your mother? How did she react?"

"She stood by my father's decision. She always had."

"Your parents sound like a loving couple," I said.

"They were. They loved and trusted each other, and they loved and trusted me. I was very lucky. Other parents would have chased George away, but they did not. They knew George was right for me. Despite their urge to keep me at home, they knew my prince had arrived."

"How was the wedding arranged, and who got to decide where the wedding was going to be held?" Siren asked.

"My mother insisted that the wedding be held in Kiev, but his mother wanted the official ceremony to be in the States. Pleasing both sides was not easy. George and I had to make some very tough choices. We wanted it to be a happy event for everyone, and the only way to solve the dilemma was having two weddings, one in Kiev and one right here in Minnesota."

"What about the travel documents? Didn't it take long to process the paperwork?" Siren asked.

"George was able to cut through much of the bureaucratic red tape and expedite the visa process using his father's political connections. Before I knew it, I was on a boat to America. It was a refreshing change and an exciting time. America was in the jazz age. There was pure jazz and its unending variants of European operetta fusion. There was Mickey Mouse and the appetite for anything electronic. But the excitement was short lived. The Great Depression took over not long after, but even the Great Depression did not last. President Roosevelt took power, and his vision and confidence brought hope back to this great country."

"What was George doing once he got back to the States?" I asked.

"All of his life, George was surrounded by lawyers, politicians, and diplomats. He was groomed to be the next U.S. senator of the great state of Minnesota, but instead, he went against all advice and took his chance in a totally different route. He turned down a highly sought after political position in Washington to start his own business."

"It must not have been easy to make such a life changing decision," I said. "How did his father react?"

"He did not approve, but there was nothing that he could do to stop George. With a reasonable sum of money he saved up from his grandfather's generous endowments and his own earnings, George bought his first warehouse. It was a broken-down warehouse in an abandoned part of town. He put a fresh coat of paint on it, cleaned the place up, and sold it for a profitable sum. He then went about and bought another one. Again, he renovated it and sold it off to the highest bidder. Then by a stroke of luck, World War II broke out. George decided to pool all his savings in another venture, building a startup to sell military supplies to the Allies. But that was another story." Nadia handed me an ear of corn.

"It sounds like George was quite an entrepreneur. How did he find the time to do anything else, with his busy schedule?" I asked.

Nadia laughed. "George always found time. Time was never an issue. The question you should be asking is how he spent it. When it came to using his spare time, it always boiled down to either me or the silly car his father had given him as a wedding gift."

"Do you mean the 1906 Renault that's at the front of the house?"

"Yes. How did you know it is a 1906 Renault?" Nadia asked.

"Victor knows everything about that car. His family has one stored in their garage," Siren said.

"It's one of the finest cars made during the first decade of the century," I said. "It has a powerful Oldsmobile single-cylinder engine."

"I am afraid I do not know much about cars," Nadia said. "To be honest, I have not paid much attention to that thing."

"Back then, only the wealthy could afford such an elegant item. It cost about three times the price of a house. The entire body was impeccably put together including its round-corner single-limousine coachwork, leather upholstery, and hood catch."

"You and George would have gotten along. He cared for that car like it was his own son. Every Sunday after church he spent hours polishing that thing. All the parts had to be spotless; otherwise he refused to do anything else for the rest of the afternoon. At times he paid more attention to that silly object than to me."

"Is that why you left it out in the rain?" Siren asked.

"George and I quarreled on numerous occasions over that car." Nadia smirked. "That car had its glory days, but it is pay back time."

"What did George do on his free time beside polishing his car?" Siren asked.

"He read. George loved to read. It was a good thing, because I loved to read, too. We spent days and months combing through his large collection of books. His passion for literature was not an acquired taste. George was born to read. He also was born to teach. You would assume that a man with his busy schedule would lack the patience to teach little old me, but not George. He took his time. He explained and clarified everything."

Nadia curled forward and lowered her head.

"What's wrong?" Siren asked.

"Memories are all you have when you are my age," Nadia said. "Everything else slowly ceases to exist. One day, these memories will be gone, too."

"Don't say that. You'll always remember George," Siren said.

Nadia looked outside. The drizzle started again.

"I think about George a lot," Nadia said. "The rain reminds me of him. We spent a lot of time in the rain working on our tomato garden. Uprooting weeds is much easier when the soil is wet. Rainwater softened the earth. You should have seen us. We plucked away like two little kids. We had mud on our fingers and toes."

"It sounds fun," I said.

"It was. I never had so much fun. Grownups rarely play in the rain. George and I did. It was a special thing. George taught me not to take life too seriously. He said that life is too short to be stiff. 'Don't you worry too much about what other people think,' he said. I took that message to the heart."

I felt something beneath the table. Storm sat on the floor with his mouth open. The puckish face reminded me that of a spoiled child. His eyes blinked incessantly. I tossed a chunk of biscuit. He snatched the food midair and nibbled on it like a horse. Within seconds, it was gone. He begged for more. I tossed another piece. Again, he ingested the food swiftly.

"Stop feeding the dog," Siren warned in her conspiratorial whisper. Her gaze returned to Nadia. "George must have been a great husband," she said.

"He was a wonderful husband and a caring human being. He had an amazing ability to calm my worries and fears. He was also a mentor and a friend. I was his young apprentice, naive at the trade of life. Like a guardian angel, he protected me, guided me with love, filled my mind with knowledge, and always made sure I had enough to eat. On our thirtieth anniversary we went on a road trip to North Carolina. George took me to a nice country restaurant for the famous southern ribs. After the meal, he ordered me a strawberry sundae. I warned him not to feed me too much, or I would get fat. Do you know what he told me?"

"What?" Siren asked.

"He said, 'Eat. I don't care if you're three hundred pounds. I'll still love you.' He remained true to his words until the day he died."

"George sounds much like my grandfather," I said. "Growing up, my father used to tell me stories of how Grandpa Antonin encouraged Grandma Marie to eat and not worry about her weight."

"Antonin is not a common American name," Nadia said.

"He was a first generation immigrant like yourself. In fact, had Grandpa Antonin lived, he would be about your age. He was born on May 1, 1910."

"Where was he born, if I may ask?" Nadia asked.

"The Prague District of the Czechoslovakia Republic. He also studied medicine in Charles University in Prague."

"That was a prestigious university back then and still is today. Do you know that Charles the Fourth founded it in 1348?"

"That's interesting. I didn't know that," I said.

"It formed the medical triangle of Berlin, Vienna, and Prague in the eighteenth, nineteenth, and twentieth centuries," Nadia said.

"How did your grandfather meet your grandmother?" Siren asked.

"They met in the army. After spending six years in medical school, Grandpa Antonin joined the Army Medical Service of the Territorial Army Headquarters in Prague. It was there that he met Grandma Marie."

"Was she a soldier, too?" Siren asked me. She then turned her head toward Nadia and said, "Victor's dad is a four-star general."

"Oh, really?" Nadia reacted in surprise.

I continued, "Grandma Marie was not a soldier. She was the daughter of a colonel of the Army Medical Service. I could see why Grandpa Antonin was madly attracted to Grandma Marie. She was not only gorgeous, but also brilliant. Fluent in Russian, Latin, French, Italian, German, Czech, and English, Grandma Marie could command an intelligent conversation with any man."

"She sounds like my George," Nadia said.

"Grandma Marie was no ordinary woman. She would have been the next Nobel Laureate for her world-renowned work in cancer research, had it not been for her unexpected death."

"What happened?" Nadia's curiosity pigued.

"She was on her way to a lecture at the Wistar Institutes in Philadelphia. A drunk driver bulldozed his pickup truck into Grandma Marie's sedan and drove her car into a concrete wall."

Nadia gasped. "That's horrible!"

"It was a tragic death and a great loss for the scientific community. Grandma Marie was, at the time, one of the early pioneering scientists exploring an alternative cancer treatment to replace surgical procedures or chemotherapy. More specifically, she and a team of scientists conducted experiments exploring new ways to induce immune defense against cancer growth."

"How did she get into this field in the first place? Did your grandfather have anything to do with it or did her father influence her into doing what she did?"

"I guess both men played some minor role in contributing to her career decision, but here's what really happened: She had always wanted to become a doctor, an American doctor, but meeting Grandpa Antonin pushed her plan a few years back. She was thrilled when the news finally came of her acceptance into the University of Pennsylvania School of Medicine."

"That's one of America's oldest and most distinguished medical institutions," Nadia said. She cleared her throat and turned her attention back to me. "I am sorry. You were saying—"

"The day Grandma Marie left Prague, Grandpa Antonin gave her a warm hug and sent her on her way halfway across the world not realizing what he had done."

"What?" Siren gaped.

"There was an unborn child in her uterus. That unborn child was my father, the great American general."

"That's so neat," Siren said. She addressed Nadia. "Victor never told me anything about his family history."

"That's because you never ask," I rebutted. "I thought you weren't interested."

"Who told you I wasn't interested?"

"Can we get back to the story?" Nadia asked.

I continued, "In medical school Grandma Marie attended classes until she could not do so. On January 4, 1934, my father was born."

"How long did she take for maternity leave?" Siren asked.

"Two weeks."

"That's all?"

"Yeah, she was one tough cookie. In fact, Grandpa Antonin once told me that she single-handedly tended to the needs of her newborn, my father, and attended class at the same time. She was determined to finish medical school. Her determination drew admiration from a fellow classmate, a former American scientist turned physician she referred to as James. James talked Grandma Marie into meeting some of his former German and Czech colleagues."

Siren interrupted. "Let me guess. This fortuitous encounter with James helped your Grandma Marie realize that her talents were not in dissecting the human body but in discovering the enigma that it holds."

"Very good!" I said. "It looks like someone has been paying attention."

"I am not sure what you two are talking about," Nadia said.

"Grandma Marie was fascinated by the causes of diseases on a microscopic level and what measures could be taken to prevent diseases, so she pursued her career in medical research and dedicated her life to finding cures for cancer."

"There must be hundreds of scientists out there in the world," Siren said. "What made her so special?"

"Her work in immunology and immunotherapy was thirty years ahead of its time. Her contributions later carried her around the globe. She conducted research in Europe, Asia, and Africa as well as presenting at national and international scientific conferences around the world. Her distinguished record earned her a tenured position in the Research Triangle of North Carolina. She sponsored Grandpa Antonin over, saving him from a potential blow in the outbreak of World War II."

"That's a wonderful story," Nadia said.

The grandfather clock struck twelve with a loud clang.

"Oh, dear. It is already midnight," Nadia said.

"I think I better call it a night." I yawned. It had been a long drive, and Siren and I were ready for bed.

Chapter 24

OLD GEORGE WATCHING

NADIA LED SIREN AND ME UPSTAIRS. Thirty or so years ago Nadia would have climbed the steps with great ease, but that was no longer the case. Time had taken a great toll on her body. It had shriveled her muscles and weakened her joints. No longer young and toned, she fought her way up the winding staircase. Siren and I offered to help, but she insisted that she was fine. A step at a time, she made it to the top.

Siren and I followed her into the guest bedroom, a large room covered with murals and columns carved with exquisite, radiant-red detailing. The room was filled with attractive objects, including yellow-eyed dolls, lace pillows, antique cabinets, a classic wall clock with winding laurel leaves, and a tapestry-draped bed. On the wall in between a cross-shaped window facing the door were two paintings in ornate frames. The one on the left showcased the story of forbidden love on the Turret Stairs. The one on the right portrayed a beautiful French courtesan lounging on a bed and bathing in the sunlight. Beneath the window was a Victorian fainting couch with a detached pillow roll.

"You two can sleep here," Nadia said. She pointed to a king-size bed where she and George used to sleep.

"Look at this place," I whispered. "This must be George's personal fuck chamber."

"Shut up!" Siren shushed.

"What? It's true. Look around us."

Siren's gaze wandered. She studied the rare frescoes, the linen, the mahogany veneer, and a tree outside. "That's a colossal tree," she said, walking toward the window.

I joined Siren by the window and so did Nadia.

"It is a sycamore," Nadia said. "It must be over a hundred years old. It has been there for as long as I can remember." It was a tall tree with thorny branches. It bulged from the earth and clawed at the world like fingers catching rain. Solid as a rock, the tree stood mighty and relentless against nature's wrath. It had survived the raging rain, the frigid snow, the blustery wind, and the scorching heat. It remained firm, robust, and breathing as mortals withered, decayed, and died away. Attached to its limb was an old swing, a chipped pine board strung together by two pieces of oxidized chains. On the same tree limb at a window-view level was a sable bird. Wing folded, the creature traversed back and forth with the gushing wind. Farther out behind the sycamore a lake loomed. An eerie stillness hung over the lake. Dusky and shrouded, its surface appeared to siphon water from the darkened sky. Nadia pointed. "That is Lake Mirror. George and I used to swim in it every summer. He loved to pick me up and toss me into the water from the top of that large boulder in the shape of a thumb that arched over the lake." Nadia distanced herself from the window and walked to an antique cabinet next to the bathroom door. She removed a clean set of towels from its drawer and returned our direction. "One for you and one for you," Nadia said, handing Siren and me each a towel. "If you two need anything else, just holler."

"I'm sure we'll be fine, thank you," Siren said.

"Goodnight." Nadia made her way out of the room and walked toward the stairs. The door creaked to a partial close.

"Don't you find this place odd?" I asked.

"What do you mean?" Siren responded.

"Look around us. If this is Nadia and George's old bedroom as she claimed, how come there are no pictures of them together?"

"There's a portrait of her on the cabinet."

"Yeah, but where is George? Come to think of it, isn't it strange that there's not a single photo of George anywhere in the house?"

"Maybe she doesn't like to be reminded of the past."

"That's nonsense. Maybe old George simply didn't exist. She probably made him up to amuse us."

"Why would she do such a thing?"

"I don't know."

"She couldn't have made the whole thing up. It's impossible. If she made George up, who brought her to America? And how did she end up with this huge estate?"

"Perhaps she murdered George and inherited his fortune."

"Now you're being plain silly. If she murdered him, she wouldn't have spoken so fondly of him."

"Then why would she abandon this bedroom and settle for the one downstairs? It's much bigger here, and it has a better view."

"Did you see the way she groaned on the way up here? She is too old to climb those steps."

"I think old George died in this room. That's why she moved out."

"Stop it!" Siren responded. "This place already gives me the creeps."

"Come on, you don't believe in old George looking over your shoulder tonight, do you?"

"What makes you so sure? Look at this place."

"It's all in your head. There's no ghost or goblin."

"That's what you think," Siren said. "Just because you haven't seen one doesn't mean there isn't one. Have I ever told you what happened to Joseph?"

"Oh no, not another Bible fable."

"I'm talking about Anna's father, dummy."

"What happened to Joseph? Did he die while making love to his wife?"

"You're such a jerk! What is it with you men? Everything is about sex. Can't you get it out of your mind for a minute?"

"Okay, there's no point in getting all riled up for nothing. My ears are yours. Tell me your story. Tell me what happened to Moses," I said.

"It's Joseph."

"Okay, Joe with a beard and a cane."

"You're hopeless."

"Are you going to tell your story or not?"

"I will if you stop interrupting."

"Go ahead. I'm listening."

"It was a humid summer night," Siren began. "Anna's mother, Natalia, was out of town. Joseph had the house to himself. He was having problems falling asleep, so he lay in bed tossing and turning. Around four in the morning, he heard something. It sounded like hands brushing against straw."

"It was probably the wind," I said.

"It couldn't have been the wind. It was a calm night. The tree was still, and the leaves were silent."

"What about rats? They make noises."

"There were no rats in the house. Joseph thought it was his wife. He thought Natalia had returned from her trip from out of town. He called out to her, but she didn't answer. The thing, whatever it was, just hovered before his eyes like a piece of white pajamas strung to a clothes line."

"What did he do?"

"He dipped his hand into a porcelain water bowl next to his bed and wet his face. He looked again."

"Let me guess, the object remained."

"Yes, it dangled in midair. Joseph grabbed the water bowl and threw at it. Water splattered everywhere. The object disappeared."

"Did Joseph think he saw a ghost?"

"A nonbeliever like you, he tried to come up with the most logical explanation. He blamed it on the summer heat and his lack of sleep. He believed they caused him to see things at odd hours."

"He was probably right."

"But that didn't explain the series of incidents that followed. Natalia started acting up. She talked in her sleep. She stripped and walked around the house naked in the middle of the night. She wailed 'Death is near! Death is near!' A day after, Natalia's body was found dangling from a tree with a coil around her neck. It was the same tree in the orchard where her mother had died."

"What did Joseph think?"

"He said his wife simply went crazy. He thought she had eaten something wrong from the day before, something that poisoned her mind and made her delusional."

"Joseph could be right. He was smart not to connect coincidental happenings with superstitious belief. It was very possible that his wife did eat something that caused her to act the way she acted. Remember the Salem witch hunts during the early days? Girls were accused of being possessed by the devil. In reality, it was the ergot in the cereal grains the girls consumed that caused them to convulse and see witches and apparitions."

"But how do you explain this?" Siren asked. "After Natalia's death, Joseph and Anna continued to reside in the same house that his grandfather had built. Joseph tended his crops and raised his herds. On weekends he sold his farm produce in the local market with Anna's help. The routine cycle repeated itself from week to week. Then, a year and thirteen days later, another woman walked into Joseph's life. She was a widow from a nearby town. Wearing a black hat, the widow approached Joseph's produce stand. She snuck glances at him while she picked over his potatoes. Joseph flirted back. The widow's one-time encounter turned into a weekly visit. It didn't take long for the cordial business interactions to turn personal. Infrequent nightly visits were made to each other's houses. Joseph and the widow maintained their casual relationship for years, seeing each other only when their needs arose. Then one day, Joseph decided to make it official. He asked her to marry him, but before she moved in, Joseph wanted to redo a portion of his old house."

"Why?"

"He wanted a fresh start."

"I meant why did he want to stay in the same place?"

"I don't know. Maybe he loved that house."

"His wife died in that house. I would have moved out."

"She died in the orchard."

"What's the difference? It's still the same piece of land."

"Anyway, Joseph wanted the aging floor replaced, so he started stripping the wood. Halfway through the job, he found something. Beneath the wood was a metal panel, a tightly sealed hatch. Joseph pried the panel loose with a crowbar and ventured inside the hole in the ground."

"That's awesome! I would love to have a secret chamber right beneath my dining room floor. What was inside?"

"At the bottom of the cave was a protruding marker of some sort. Curious as to what lay beneath, Joseph got a shovel and chunked away the earth until he struck something. A woody sound echoed. He chunked again. Something showed. He gave one hard blow. A casket door broke open."

"Gold!"

"No, bones and human remains. They were those of a man, a woman, and a small child. It appeared all three were brutally murdered. Their jaws were shattered and skulls punctured."

"What did Anna think of Joseph's finding?"

"She didn't say. But she said Joseph dismissed as coincidental the connection between the mutilated bodies he found and the other events that had occurred."

"Good for him."

"I think it's a family curse."

"That's absurd. A curse on who?"

"Joseph and anyone connected to Joseph, for the murder of those poor souls. Look at what happened to Natalia. She also died a bizarre death. It was as if something possessed her mind and forced her to kill herself."

"There're no ghosts or spirits out there bantering around us," I said. "There is only us, walking and breathing human beings made of flesh and blood. When we die, that's it. It's over. Whatever unworldly event Joseph saw was probably a byproduct of an ill mind, like those women in Salem."

I walked Siren into the bathroom. Nadia had left the water running. We undressed and submerged ourselves in the tub. The water rose. Ripples emerged. We washed ourselves and went to bed. Ghost or no ghost, Siren and I slept well that night.

Chapter 25

STORM'S BARKS

THE MORNING ARRIVED with Storm's barks. Nadia sent him for our wake up call. He squatted on his hind and barked away until Siren and I crawled out of bed and followed him downstairs. Nadia was already in the kitchen finishing up her chores.

"Good morning," Nadia said, slicing an orange in half. "Did you two sleep well?"

"I did," Siren said.

"What about you, Victor?" Nadia asked.

"I was up part of the night," I said.

"Was the room too hot?"

"The temperature was fine. There were breezes from the window."

"Then what kept you up?"

"Every time I travel and have to sleep in a hotel or someone else's house, it usually takes me a night to adjust to the new smell or feel of things."

"I am the same way," Nadia said. "When I was a child my mother had to bring my favorite pillow along whenever we went on a road trip. If not, I would be up all night."

"Isn't it amazing how our mind works?" Siren asked. "Even at the depths of unconsciousness, it's still aware of unfamiliarity."

"That's an awfully insightful statement coming from someone who snored the night away," I said.

"I didn't snore, you liar!"

"I'm kidding. Siren is like a puppy when she sleeps. She curls to the side and stays there without making a sound."

Nadia finished squeezing the oranges and joined us at the table. Like a mother preparing her children for the first day of school, she poured Siren and me each a glass of orange juice and filled our plates with English muffins, French toast, scrambled eggs, and Italian sausages.

"What are you waiting for, dear?" Nadia said. "Eat! The food is getting cold."

"Did you make these muffins?" Siren asked.

"Yes, dear," Nadia said.

"They're so good! I haven't had one this good since third grade when Ms. Johnson brought the class her famous cranberry muffins."

"I am glad you like it. I want to start things right for you two. A good breakfast is essential for your tough road ahead." Nadia placed a napkin on her lap. "How do you feel about this door-to-door thing? Are you nervous?"

"A little," Siren said.

"I heard horror stories. You two ought to be careful."

"I'm sure we'll be fine," I said. "Countless students have done it before us. If worse comes to worst, we'll pack up and leave."

"What do you mean, we?" Siren asked. "I'm not going home until the summer ends."

"Now, now, dear. There is no point in arguing this early in the morning."

"She's right," I said. "We should conserve our energy for later. We'll have plenty of opportunity to run our mouths in the weeks to come."

"Where are you two off to this morning?" Nadia asked.

"Saint Clouds," Siren said.

"That is a good hour drive from here. Is that where you two will be working?"

"No. We're going there to meet our boss and the rest of the sales team. We'll be assigned our specific sales location during the meeting."

"Will you be back for dinner?"

"We don't know yet," Siren said. "Victor and I still have to pick up our sales permit," Siren said.

"Peddling without proper registration or direct sales license in some areas is illegal," I said. "And we have no plan for spending our first day at work sitting in the back seat of a police car or locked up behind bars."

"That's right," Siren agreed. "Time is money, and time wasted is money unearned."

"Siren and I also want to explore Stillwater a little and don't want to keep you waiting," I said.

"It would be no trouble. I will make dinner anyway and leave the food in the refrigerator. You can warm it up in the microwave when you come back."

Nadia told us more about herself. She talked about George and his family. She even talked about Storm and the type of food he liked. A master narrator, she filled her tales with unexpected twists and turns. She talked until we told her that we had to leave. She went to her room and brought us George's spare set of house keys, one for each lock.

Chapter 26

DOORS HERE WE COME

S IREN AND I SPENT our first week working in a small town about a twenty-minute drive from Still-water. Early each morning before sunrise, we took a cold shower and tiptoed out of the house. Not even Storm heard us leave. By 7:15 a.m., we entered our favorite breakfast place, Big Joe, and had Marie-Anne bring us our regular: two large pancakes, and a giant omelet filled with ham, green peppers, mushroom, potato and onion. Siren liked her omelet with ketchup, and Marie-Anne brought out the ketchup, too. After the hardy meal, we hit the road.

Reality caught up with Siren and me on the fifth day in the field. It became apparent that my father's words confirmed my worst fear. I was no salesman, and neither was Siren. In a week we acquired two orders valued at sixty dollars each. Thank goodness there was Nadia to save the day. She packed Siren and me lunch and made us dinner. We would have starved, had it not been for her. Siren and I had high expectations. We did not anticipate or accept such poor performance. Two sales were justifiable for a day of work, but not for a week in the field. House after house, rejections punched us in the face. "I am not interested" was the excuse. Our confidence was chipped away with each door slam, but the threats and disappointments did not deter us. Siren and I marched on. Our pride and livelihood were at stake. We certainly did not expect to live off Nadia forever, although she had more than enough food to feed a small army.

Despite our despair, calling my father to ask for money would be out of the question; therefore, the only option was to push on. Rain or shine, Siren and I went from one street to the next. We marched forward carrying our black company bag heavy with demo books.

Occasionally we roamed into the wrong neighborhood and stirred up a scene. One such occasion was Hattie Lane, a tree-lined street in a community of retired elderly. Our tennis shoes made noises. The dogs growled behind each picket fence. Our footsteps grew louder. One by one, like a domino effect, they barked. In pitch darkness, their barks hounded us like flies. Windows lit, curtains pried open, and eyes peeped. Siren and I started running. We ran like we never run before, bags swinging and hands flailing.

Chapter 27

TONGUE OF GOLD

B USINESS PICKED UP the second week in the field, after Siren and I spent a day following our sales manager around. "What you learned in Nashville is only theory," Buck said. "Out in the real world, things work differently. Your talk, timing, and body language have to be right. Knowing when and how to approach a potential buyer makes the difference between making a sale and getting the door slammed in your face."

Siren and I learned our lessons the hard way, and we were determined not to repeat our mistakes. We honed our people-handling skills by studying from the master himself. We watched how Buck went about eliciting information from strangers. He used names and referrals to establish rapport. He got details from children playing in the street. When Buck walked, Siren and I followed, and when he talked, we listened. "Genuine friendliness and enthusiasm get you in doors," Buck said. "Genuine belief in the products you sell enables you to close each deal."

One door at a time, Buck showed us his bag of tricks. He pulled out his magic wand and took center stage. He hypnotized his targets with his eyes, body gestures, and words. Buck had a tongue that could turn garbage into gold. Men, women, and children savored every word that spilled from his mouth, not because they were true, but because they were mesmerizing.

"The rule of thumb is to never stand too close to the door or stand directly in front of it," Buck advised. "Always stay a step or two to the side. And don't forget to smile."

No expert psychologist in the world had taught me more about human behavior than Buck. He was a smooth-talking door-to-door salesman with a mouth sweeter than honey. Slick Buck, I named him.

Siren and I witnessed how Buck operated the first door he knocked on. It was eight o'clock on a Saturday morning. Siren and I stood two feet behind him as instructed. Buck gave a light thud on a mobile home door. There was no answer. He knocked again and stepped back and to the side. Still there was no answer. Buck stepped up and knuckled louder. An elephantine man sprang out of his trailer. Shirtless and hair flying, he looked furious. Buck calmly took a step back and smiled a big smile, a Ronald McDonald smile. The arch of his lips was wider than the Golden Gate Bridge.

"Howdy," Buck said, reaching out for a handshake. "I'm Buck."

"What do you want?" the man growled.

"I hope I didn't catch you at a bad time," Buck said. He swiftly moved to put the man at ease. Before we knew it, Buck, Siren, and I were inside the man's trailer home drinking coffee and sharing a bowl of dry Fruit Loops cereal with his five-year-old daughter and a hamster named Sam.

Chapter 28

THE HERMIT
AND THE PRIEST

S IREN AND I started the summer trudging in
neighborhoods of retirees, low-income families,
and super-rich elites. After our raw initiation into
the sales business, Buck reassigned us to better locations.
They included the sprawling suburban settings where
moms and dads had the financial backing to enrich their
children's education, even if it meant having to spend a
few extra dollars on a door-to-door salesman's products.
Unlike the lower income communities where parents
were too poor to buy anything for their children but the
bare essentials or the upper-class communities where kids
already had everything they needed, the middle-class
communities were just right. In these communities, each
house was a potential gold mine. Despite their lucrative
appeal, before long, Siren and I ran out of houses to

approach and had to venture elsewhere for other doors to knock.

Working in the township areas was a welcome change. The farms, brooks, trees, and raw country air were all good for the body and mind. Most living quarters—designed to keep the interior cool during the summer and warm during the winter—were Scandinavian. Their occupants had long Norwegian last names. One house in particular stood out vividly. It was a timeworn timbered shanty buried against a hill. Located behind an unmarked road in the township of St. Joseph County, the wintry structure with a tin roof that protruded a child's height above the ground nearly escaped my sight. I would have driven past it, had it not been for a rusty blue pickup truck rigged with plywood boards parked by the side of the road. When I spotted the truck, I pulled Pixie over for a look. Siren and I ventured down a cobbled path that wedged into the earth. A few steps closer revealed a dilapidated staircase that led to a weed-tangled door.

I inhaled and thumped on the door. A Viking-like hermit in rags crept from his cave. His blackened teeth, foot-long beard, and foul smell sent Siren fleeting back. Face hollowed and expression-numbed, the man slumped dwarf-like in front of us. His gaze wandered to a flock of cawing birds that circled the sky above a scarecrow in the cornfield. I knew I was not about to make a sale to the cadaverous hermit, but I threw my sales pitch anyway, for practice sake.

"Good afternoon," I said.

The hermit cut me off. "Go away."

"I apologize for stopping by uninvited, but I have only a few minutes to spare."

"What do you want?" he asked, frowning in distrust.

"My name is Victor, and this is Siren. We're college students who have been talking to families in the area about these study guides for young children." I showed him my demo books.

"I'm not interested. Can't you see there aren't any kids around here?" the man asked in inhospitable monotony.

"What about those swings behind the broken tractor?" I pointed toward the cornfield.

Detecting my resolve to stay, the man stepped out of hiding and walked Siren and me down a dirt path.

"My wife left me years ago," he said.

"I'm terribly sorry," Siren said.

"What for? That woman drove me crazy. Day in and day out, she nagged. She was never satisfied with anything. I gave her all I had, and she still wanted more."

We approached the abandoned swing. The hermit perused his surroundings and touched the swing. Cracked paint spun earthbound.

"It has been a long time since I set foot out here," the hermit said. "Billy used to play here. He used to spend hours on this swing."

"Where is he now?"

"He's with his mother. She stole him from me." The man dropped to his knees and sobbed.

"Don't cry," Siren said, holding the man's shoulder.

"Do you know what it's like to lose a child?" he asked, wiping the tears from his eyes. "Do you know what it's like to lose everything you worked so hard for?"

I had no answer for him; neither did Siren. We could only imagine the depth of his pain. There was no greater punishment for a man than to be left alone in a world that was once filled with hope and joy. With the tick of a clock hand, all was taken away. His mushroomed hair, bewildered eyes, spiraling fingernails, and rail-thin frame eloquently conveyed what he failed to say in words. Siren and I knew he was happy once, a long time ago, but like all things, love was transitory. We knew that the hermit would die alone and brokenhearted. Bit by bit time would continue to wash him thin. The loneliness would consume him, and he would suffer long after all the corn was gone and the crows had died.

The hermit talked about an old priest who lived in a yellow plantation-style house next to an abandoned church a mile down the road in a town called Annandale. I remembered the church the hermit described, a solitary building with unwashed Venetian glass windows, simple woodcarvings, and intriguing icons. It was a white church that nudged palely against a raging sky. The seasoned edifice blended into the formation of the elements and symbolized man's struggle against time. It was a small church with a remarkably tall wooden cross at the top. Sitting at the edge of the world where the ground was flat, the dilapidated structure yawned at the end of another day. The epic of the hermit's life was once held in that church. Within the confines of its ancient walls the man and his wife met and got married. In that sacred fortress in a distant past, he felt the power of his so-called God. There, he claimed, his soul had been saved and washed clean of sin. In that church, he experienced the magic of life.

Siren and I discovered the church and met its caretaker on a stormy day. Forced to stop by the wind and rain, we scurried the priest's way. He sat impeccably dressed on a rocking chair with a cane on his lap. Under a yellow front porch awning, he nibbled an ear of corn. Oak-fired and oven fresh, the corn looked mighty fine for a rainy day.

"Good afternoon." The priest greeted us with a proud head up.

"How do you do?" I hailed.

"Quite a storm, isn't it?"

"It sure is."

"The good Lord finally brings us rain." He smiled. His two gold teeth showed and so did a yellow kernel stuck in between.

"We can always use some rain," I said.

The priest tipped his bifocals and squinted into the rain. "That's a fine machine you got there."

"We call her Pixie," Siren said.

"Dixie. What kind of name is that?" The priest snickered.

"It's Pixie. P-I-X-I-E."

"Pixie, huh? What kind of name is Pixie?"

"What's the matter? Don't you like it?"

"I like it fine, but I have never thought to name my truck Roy."

"Pixie is a good car," Siren said. "She takes good care of us."

"Yeah, she was pretty good until the storm took her wipers off," I added. "Now she's blind as a bat."

The priest laughed. "You kids talk like that car is alive."

"Pixie is one of us," Siren said. "She has more heart than most people we know."

"You think we're crazy, don't you?" I asked.

"No, I think you two have too much time on your hands," the old priest said.

Inside the priest's house two white cats snoozed away on a tattered living room couch. They seemed content with each other's company and pleased by the cool breeze. "Cats are lazy creatures," Siren once said. "All they do is sleep all day. They sleep when it rains and sleep when it snows. They sleep on the couch, on the floor, on the bed, and even on the window ledge." Clearly, those two white cats were no exception. They slept without the slightest care in the world. They slept as the priest spoke.

"Life wasn't easy being the son of a ranger," the priest said. "Growing up, my brother and I used a team of horses hooked to a hay wagon to feed hay to the livestock. There was always work to do on the ranch. My father fixed broken trucks and tractors. My brother reopened water gaps in the winter. I spent most of my time training young horses. Mom did the cooking. When one chore was completed, another awaited us. At the end of the day everyone gathered around the dinner table for a good meal. I could never get enough of Mom's cooking. I loved the smell of logs burning from her wooden stove. After each meal, my brother and I gathered in front of the fireplace and played poker."

The rain continued to pour and the priest talked more about his past. He talked about those days when his church was packed with worshippers. The hermit's name was mentioned. "He was a sharp looking young man when I first met him." The priest recalled. "He was polite, bright, and charming. The ladies loved him. One, in particular, he was attracted to, a beautiful redhead with a light complexion. He approached her after church. They hit it off quite well. Two months later, he proposed to her."

Siren and I left the priest's house after the rain stop. Before we left, he suggested that we should go see his great grand nephew. "Little Timmy might be interested in one of your books," the priest said.

Timmy lived in St. Joseph Township. He was trout fishing at a nearby stream when I first saw him the day after Siren and I left the priest's house. I did not know the boy was Timmy until I saw him again two days later at his father's farm. He was sprinkling birdseed for a flock of colorful chickens in his front yard when Siren and I stopped by.

"How come the chickens aren't fenced in?" I asked.

"Them suckers won't run away," Timmy replied. "They usually return to the barn when the sun sets." He sounded quite knowledgeable on chicken habits for a boy his age, probably no older than seven.

"Has anybody ever tried to steal them?" Siren asked.

"Not really. Only the foxes and owls come after them. Several summers back, Daddy used to have over a hundred of them little suckers running around. One night about eighty of them disappeared."

"What happened?" Siren asked.

"The owls snatched them off."

"How do you know the owls stole your daddy's chickens?" I asked.

Timmy scratched his head. "Daddy killed ten of them with his shotgun. Bang! Bang! Bang! They all dropped dead. And along came a chicken, flopping and making noises of all kinds."

"What about foxes? Did your daddy shoot them, too?"

"No. That's the geese's job. Do you see them geese over there?" He pointed to a flock that clustered around a mud puddle.

"They'll give the foxes a good chase if they dare to come around. They'll even come after you and your car, too."

"Is your daddy home?" I asked.

"Yes, he's inside."

"Can you call him out here for a second?"

Timmy ran to the screen door and hollered. "Daddy! Daddy! Come out here!"

Siren and I met up with Timmy's father. We showed him and Timmy a set of children's books. Timmy was more interested in his flock of chickens than the books, but his father ordered a set anyway because the priest had made the referral. I closed the deal and drove to the next house half a mile down the dirt road.

Chapter 29

SUMMER RAIN

THE RAIN FELL LATE the day summer ended. Up in the sky scattered clouds thickened into a black haze. Soon there was nothing but total darkness. A trickle slipped from the sky. Another followed. And another. A massive downpour began. Goblet-like drops splattered the rooftop and slithered to the ground. Lightning flashed dangerously overhead. The wind wheezed and beat mercilessly on the dinging chimes. Tied to the stair pole, Storm dug low to the floor and growled. Thunder boomed. He snapped to his feet and gave out a fierce bark. More thunder smashed. He snarled, teeth showing, gnashed at his own shadow, and circled the stairs. A third time thunder deafened. Storm scrambled for the door, only to be brought back on his hind legs by the dog collar around his neck.

Behind the propped door inside Nadia's old bedroom, candlelight lit the perimeter of the floor. George's old record spun. Back facing the mirror, Siren tossed her hair aside and threw me an observant glance. Seductive, intriguing, and beguilingly powerful, she charmed me with her moves. Her low-cut gown unveiled a pair of towering legs. They spread scissor shaped in perfect symmetry. Objects of every man's desire, these remarkable legs teased my mind and tempted me to reach out and touch them. I wished to draw her near and run my hands up those legs. I wanted to mount myself on her and explore her mountains, craters, valleys, and rugged highlands. I desired to plunge into her sea and be submerged in the sacred water where the fiery furnace lay. In the core of her sun, the key to the continuing existence and evolution of man, we would harness the haze of our particles and recreate the first blistering moments of life. Bodies fused and minds united, we would light up the sky and radiate enough energy to run power grids around the world. Who said that the universe began billions of years ago when a great cloud of gas and dust collapsed in on itself under the force of its own gravity? The universe began with the collapse of a man's body on a woman's.

The candles burned. The music sounded. Desire unfolded and uncertainty hung on with stinging tenacity. I glanced prudently at the woman before me. Hands washed, hair combed, and expression relaxed, I made my way across the room.

"May I?" I beckoned an invitation with both arms.

"Of course, darling," Siren responded, lips temptingly moist.

Arms hooked and body locked, I kept an even pace. Outside, a raven swooped from the sky. It clawed onto the swaying branch of the tall sycamore and drew its ruffled wings to a close. It remained immobile behind the cross-shaped window piercing me with its devilish eyes. Two different creatures of the same world, we each had different desires. It probably wished to be inside where it was warm and dry. I wished to be free, free like the bird and hold its gift of flight. If I had wings, I would fly. I would fly somewhere far. I would fly away to some country where the weather always stayed warm and people were friendly. I would fly to the edge of a garden-lined cliff that overlooked the blue sea. As my mind remained in flight, I stroked Siren's back.

"Um, that feels good," she murmured.

Lightning flashed. Wind whipped. Trees bopped. Siren appeared to find comfort in the unsettling storm. Its imminence and ferocity aroused her in strange ways and stimulated her in untold manners. I felt the heat unleashed from her body. Its scintillating energy circled her. A bead of sweat escaped her neck and coursed down the length of her back. Sangfroid face, I continued to pace. I moved a foot forward and a foot back. Our steps synchronized.

"Do you want to hear a story?" I asked.

"Yes."

"There once lived a great warrior. After a long day in the battlefield, he returned to his campground, entered his tent, and found a beautiful woman inside. He had no idea who she was or where she came from, but he did not care. Sitting cross-legged and eyes closed, the woman remained deep into her breathing. The warrior shed his armor, retired his sword, and approached her. 'What're you doing, honey?' he asked. 'Shush!' the woman replied. 'Don't shush me,' the warrior said. Barbarian that he was, the warrior tackled the woman to the ground and shackled her crucifix style. 'Screw whatever you're doing, Baby. I want some of your famous omelet tonight.'"

"Is that what you want?" Siren asked.

"Yes, baby," I said, lowering her to the floor. "I want your homemade omelet tonight."

Lightning flashed. Thunder rolled. The rain continued to pour. Our lips touched, our tongues swirled, and out she went. Give and take away was Siren's power over men. She pleased, she taunted, she enticed, she seduced, and she destroyed all in one act. Crouched on the hardwood floor with the warmth of her buttocks against my abdomen, she began to unknot her hair. The strings came loose, and so were those on her matching nightgown. Her emerald green eyes, darkened by the charcoal night, glowed like those of a hungry cat. They wanted my flesh. They wanted me raw and wanted me fast.

Siren reached, grabbed my penis, held it tight, and began to move. Up and down it went. In a semi-mystical state of mind, I felt a torrent charging up the dried riverbed, and my emotions ran away. The infusion of blood dimmed my thought. No longer able to bear the swell, I unleashed the caged beast in me and freed myself of her grip. I embraced her bosom with my mouth and maneuvered on top. My fingers crawled up her legs and made their way inside her secret garden, a sacred temple that housed man since the birth of time. She wiggled in an attempt to break free, but this time there was no escape. All exits were sealed. All entrances blocked. In a cave without light the blind snakes ruled. And there were five. They groped, twisted, and twirled within the confine of her temple walls. Quiet, cozy, and inviting, the pulpy walls thickened with blood. They clamped tightly around my fingers and grew moist with each invasive stroke. She wriggled and squirmed. She yelped and groaned. She screeched as slaughtered for an evening meal. She was being slaughtered, and I was the slayer, the hungry Leo and a mindless beast.

Refusing to yield, Siren frantically clawed and thrashed. Teeth clenched and eyes closed, she summoned all will to prevail, but the empowering force was too great. The ravenous predator in me had roared. Nothing in the world could set her free, not even her God.

Outmatched in size and strength, Siren finally succumbed. Intoxicating perfume emanated from her flesh. Her heart raced, and her chest rose and fell. The heat from her mouth expelled. I licked sweat off her skin. It tasted like the salty ocean we swam in. With her legs pried apart, I slid inside and secured a perfect fit. Strapped together as we were, like two birds in a cage, my flesh rubbed hers. Nerves flared, sensations flickered with flames, and tingles consumed my consciousness. Bodies unified, I rode the wet tunnel. In and out of the muddy tunnel I slid. The gate of her forbidden shrine flapped. It felt good to be a part of someone, divine to be an integral part of the whole and be unified in mind and flesh. Life, energy, substance, and fluidity all combined into one.

In the heat of passion, when a woman could be no closer to a man, Siren found herself. The fragmented mind fused into one. Frightened by the thought of losing control, she resumed her struggle. "Please stop," she begged and moaned with her eyes closed. Her head shook left and right. Her mouth continued to murmur in a dreamy state, as if talking to herself in her sleep, but her body held on tight, not wanting to let go. It wanted more.

I felt her body's desire with each orgasmic reflex. I knew "no" meant "yes," so I refused to let go. She must be satisfied. The empty well must be filled. Pressing hard and mouth sucking her swelling bosom, I gave it to her full throttle. The serpent lurched. She struggled to break free, but the venom had been injected, and she wanted more with each engaging thrust. Her emotion ran wild with my unrelenting power. The moving pistol continued to jab. The cannon ball burst into flame. She squealed in a final orgasm. The fire ceased, and the battle ended. She surrendered. Exhausted and satiated, Siren rolled aside and watched the rain continue to fall. The record came to its last spin: "In the eve of a heartthrob there rests an untamed beast. With the stroke of a sun's brush the beast stirs from its sleep. In the shadow of a raindrop the beast resumes its sleep. In the abyss of the beast's sleep the great unknown disrupts and creeps."

Like the thorny branches of a lifeless tree in a cold winter night, those words from the record and the whitish glow of her naked body pricked the inner edge of my mind.

Chapter 30

JOURNEY'S END

I WAS RELIEVED when our summer excursion came to an end. The reality was, Siren and I remained unharmed. We survived the car skids, the dog chases, the cops' pursuits, and other life-threatening ordeals. In two and a half months, we pushed our strength to the limit and worked the grueling schedule. In the rain and under the sweltering sun, we knocked thousands of doors. We thudded until our knuckles burned and talked until our voices gave away. From dawn until dusk, we walked the streets and pounded each door. We drove from one neighborhood to the next and met people from all walks of life. From farmers and bankers to policemen and bikers, and from schoolteachers and homemakers to prostitutes, we met them all. We treaded across five townships in two states and worked more than eighty hours each week. The countless rejections, long hours, car wrecks, mudslides, unforgiving summer heat, and anything and everything that could possibly go wrong that went wrong tempered our minds. On more than one occasion, I pondered giving up and driving back home, but Buck's words made me hold on.

"If you don't work hard now when you're young, you'll have to work a lot harder when you're old," Buck said.

Simple as that, those words pushed me on. I endured and persevered despite the anger and fear. No snarling rottweilers, crazy mothers, local cops, or crying babies could chase me out of town. I hammered fate on the toe and made it scream. When wearied of the suburban drudgeries, Siren and I retired to the countryside. Nature eased us and put our perspective back in line. We watched the rabbits and the deer, the birds and the bees, and the ponds and the trees. We watched the farmers get up before sunrise for their daily chores. We joined them at sunset for an evening meal. We milked their cows and fed their chickens. We even ate the chickens that we fed. If nothing else came out of those experiences, Siren and I learned one thing. We learned to respect the farmers that we met. Little Timmy's family was an example. They were decent people with a strong work ethic. They knew how to take care of their land. More importantly, they were down to earth, humble, and amiable. They were neither rude nor impatient like city folks.

One evening before book delivery week, Siren and I stopped by Timmy's house for a visit. Thinking that the day should be over, I knocked on his front door. The light was on, but no one answered. I knocked again and stepped aside. Still, there was no answer.

"I think he's out in the back," Siren said.

We circled the house and followed a lemon-colored shine from the barn where we found Timmy's father. He was on top of a dented pickup truck unloading bails of hay using his two strong hands. A bail at a time, he tossed the hay to the ground. His wife, Barbara, was on the receiving end. Timmy was not far away, watching two men on horseback rounding up the cattle under the moonlit sky. Wasting no time, I removed my shirt and joined Timmy's father on the truck.

"Why don't you go down and give Barbara a hand?" I insisted. "She looks like she could use a break."

Timmy's father gladly took up on the offer and relieved Barbara of her chore. Two hours later, sweaty and tired, Timmy's father invited Siren and me inside for a cold beer. Barbara served us homemade Minnesota pie while Timmy showed Siren and me his collection of toys.

Chapter 31

FAREWELL STILLWATER

A WEEK BEFORE we left Stillwater, a truckload of the books we had sold arrived. It took Siren and me an afternoon to unload them into Nadia's garage, a garage large enough for three cars. A couple of our customers across the river in Wisconsin threw Siren and me a surprise farewell party on delivery day. One of them showed us a copy of their local paper. The article read: "Prince charming from the South and his Yankee girlfriend sold books to local school children to become their company's pacesetter. With their friendly smile and a winning attitude, they won the heart of our community." Known as the coupled peddlers and solicitors, Siren and I became household names. Those who feared us in the beginning were at ease in the end. One mother even baked us brownies while her husband paid their dues.

Siren and I did okay. I conquered my greatest fear and overcame my toughest hurdle, and Siren earned enough money to pay off her credit card debt. She even managed to stash away a few extra dollars for rainy days. We were both stronger mentally and physically. The hot summer sun did us good. We had sweated a lot, walked a lot, talked a lot, and were ready for a fresh start. As far as Pixie was concerned, she too did well, considering the rough terrain she had to endure. Despite a dent here and there, she remained in remarkably good shape. I smashed Pixie into a deer while driving home on a blustery rainy night. Siren called her insurance company the following day, got Pixie appraised, and delivered her to a Stillwater body shop to get her fixed. Whether in good times or in bad, she stood by us until the very end. Siren and I thanked her for that.

Siren and I were the lucky few. We were not robbed, mugged, or seriously injured. We even had the chance to spend a mid-August afternoon tubing down Apple River in Minnesota before returning south. The water was a bit chilly, but the beer kept us warm. We floated and drank and drank and floated. We spun around on the moving rapids under the hot summer sun. After we had our last can of beer, we began our thousand-mile trip down south, back to the university.

With our book-selling days over, Siren and I could finally relax and enjoy the sun-dappled country view with its clear blue sky and miles after miles of orange fields. I drove on, thinking about the hermit, the priest, and

Nadia. I remembered Nadia and how sad she looked when Siren and I left. For two and a half months, Nadia had fed us well. From coleslaw to barbecue ribs to her famous chicken potpie, she filled us up for the next day's run. Siren and I promised we would call her. I did, but Nadia's phone was disconnected.

Part V

A TIME TO KILL

Manhattan
Washington, DC
2003

Chapter 32

VOICE OF AN ANGEL

THE VOICE, the voice that sends me to my feet, instructs me to take the Chinatown bus early next morning. "I'll be waiting at one o'clock sharp at the corner of 'I' and Sixth Streets of D.C.," the Voice says. "Look for a woman with long black hair wearing blue jeans. And don't be late."

I scramble for a pen and a legal pad. The phone clicks. "Why does it have to be the Chinatown bus?" I ask myself. "Why not a plane, train, or Greyhound bus? I am not Chinese. I cannot speak Mandarin. Who is this person with long black hair?" She did not give me a chance. She hung up before I could ask. For a moment she had me fooled. I thought she was Siren.

Should I go? Why? No, why not is the question I should be asking. I have to go. I must go. The suspense is killing me. It has been more than a decade since I last saw Siren. I owe it to myself to dig out the truth. For sanity's sake I must find out what exactly happened to her on that fateful day following our trip from Minnesota. Even if I fail in my attempt to excavate the truth, at least I will know I have tried. I will not give up without even trying. I would rather try and fail than not try at all. It is not within my nature to sit and wait. All events happen only once. I must go to D.C. and see what fate holds.

After work I go home and pack light: a small toothbrush, a pack of Spearmint gum, a handheld radio, and a change of clothes. By 2:00, I fall asleep.

"Run! Faster!" a voice in my head echoes. I circle a helical stairwell in some strange building. Others are chasing me. Footsteps close in. My heart skips. Sweat creeps through my skin. I sprint faster and race outside. At the center of the roof is a tree, the world's tallest tree on the city's tallest building. I run to the tree and claw my way up like a chameleon. I reach for a branch. The wind blows. Rivers of lights stretch far below. The tree sways. I hang on. I spin. Everything blurs. A loud noise shrieks from the sky. Its deafening shrill is too much. I let go. "Ah!"

Sweaty and breathing heavily, I wake to the ear-piercing sound of the alarm. With running sneakers in gear and backpack ready, I stand and take one last look. Am I forgetting anything? Yes. It is drizzling outside. I need my umbrella. The subway train is only a few blocks away, but there is no point in getting wet. I am ready. D.C., here I come. I race out of my riverside condo to catch the number-four uptown train. The train worms through the spaghetti tunnel and screeches to a stop.

"Brooklyn Bridge Station," the conductor announces.

I tread the empty street. The world is still asleep. The sky is sprinkling. Moisture saturates my lungs. I turn right into Worth Street. In the distance, a woman stands alone. She is doing something, but I cannot make out what. Everything blurs in the mosquito tent vista. The trickles thicken. They spray and slap my pants and jet diagonally to the adjacent asphalt road. I walk on. My grip on the umbrella tightens. The blustery wind battles on, but I refuse to let go. The woman, an aging Chinese woman, appears more visible. Eyes shut she stands erect, her stick-like frame like a grasshopper fighting the wind and rain. She pays no attention to my passing, but I know she can hear me slogging through the puddles. Up ahead is another road, Park Row. I make a left and maintain a steady pace.

I hear music. It sounds like Chinese music, the type they play in Chinese opera houses and old Chinese movies. It is slow, stringy, and sad. It sounds like someone is dying. Its edgy, cello pitch is coming from somewhere, perhaps one of those dirty-brown tenements with running cloth lines and plant pots that dot each window ledge. The music grows louder. A small group of men and women practice Tai Chi behind a wire fence. I look at them, but my mind is somewhere else, somewhere in a parallel universe of the distant past. I keep walking. The road splits. I turn into East Broadway and scuttle past graffiti-filled rollup doors. Some are bolted shut. Others are raised at half-staff. The rest are open for business.

Men in filthy white clothes hustle in and out of rectangular trucks and vans on both sides of the street. Women walk around with their inventory pad hand counting newly arrived produce. Scallions, cabbages, cucumbers, tomatoes, and melons spill over each box.

I close in on the seafood racks. My nostrils flare. Whew! It smells. Fish odors foul the air. Sea bass; flounder; shrimp; oysters; and crabs of all colors, shapes, and sizes line the ice-filled racks. Murky shoe prints layer the filthy floor.

Farther up and two doors away is a small pastry shop. Decision time. I better get something to eat. It is going to be a long ride. I enter the store. A foot from the door two roughly shaved butchers lean against the wall with their legs spread. Each is armed with a knife in his hand and a burning cigarette in his mouth. Their white aprons are stained with blood. They do not look friendly. Their eyes, dark and hawkish, follow me with distrust. New York Chinatown might be part of America, but this is their domain. A preppy white male like me does not belong here. I am treading on their territory, and they can kill me for that. The knives they are holding, the blades sharp enough to chop off hands, make me edgy. It would be foolish to get involved in a power struggle with those two men. They are big men, bigger than any Chinese men that I have ever seen. By their sheer size, I decide they must be used to killing things. I visualize them charging at me like a pair of mad bulls. All it would take is one jab from behind, and I would collapse and die without a fight. My blood would spill on the ratty floor.

In the shadowy world of New York Chinatown everything is a big disguise. Behind the fake handbag shops, the decorative jewelry stores, and the multitude of restaurants are the sweatshops, prostitution rings, and the mobs. Those two butchers could very well be members of Chinese mobs. I can tell from their cold stares, fierce look, and the green tattoos engraved on their arms that they are men not to fool around with.

On my right, idling behind a glass case, a short Chinese woman yawns. Groggy and peevish, she awaits my decision. Little white cake, brownies, crusty almond rolls, steamed dumplings, bite-size custard tarts, shrimp-stuffed eggplant, sticky rice wrapped in bamboo leaves, and sesame balls line the aluminum tray. Everything looks fresh. I must decide. "Be sure to speak slowly," I remind myself, "and whatever she says, stay calm. She looks hot-tempered." I point to a yellow cake with yellow filling and say, "I want that." All signs are in Chinese, and I do not read Chinese.

Befuddled, the woman frowns. She tucks her chin up an inch above the glass case. "What do you want?" she asks.

"That," I point again.

"Anything else?"

"Coca-Cola," I say.

That she understands.

"Is that all?"

I nod.

"One fifty."

I hand her two dollars. "Keep the change," I say. No damage done; not yet, anyway.

The traffic clears. I look up. Everything is still in Chinese, everything except the building numbers. Odd numbers are on the left and even numbers on the right. I pace steadily up the street. Head on, the front end of a bus juts from the corner of the road. A few feet from the bus three women in lily-white camises lean against a steel rollup door.

"New York, Philadelphia, D.C.!" they growl. Their voices rise an octave and their faces glow at my coming. They look like they have just seen Jesus Christ. "New York, D.C.!" One aggressively fans her roll of green tickets up close. I back off and flash my electronic receipt. Disappointed, the woman directs me to my bus, the last of four at a corner between East Broadway and Forsyth Street.

It is 7:15 a.m. I am forty-five minutes early. Stepping a foot up, I make my way into the bus. The interior is dimly lit. Clearly I am the first. Wait, there is someone. A thick bearded man in dungarees and a polo shirt stands alone in the back. Eyes narrowed with suspicion, he looks at me and disappears into the toilet stall. I resume scanning. All windows are securely shut. The air is muggy and stale. The rain slows to a stop. Sleeves rolled and umbrella folded I proceed down the narrow aisle and stop halfway. Perfect, a seat by the emergency exit. I take an aisle seat on the left. An inch above my shoulder a red metal rim latches to the window. Two rows ahead a small TV hangs from the top. Two rows behind, a young woman crouches, asleep, below a headrest. There is no one else on the bus except us three, the thick bearded man, the Indian woman, and me nibbling on the yellow cake. It tastes sweet with a lemony flavor. My throat cries for a drink, but I do not want to open the soda just yet. There is no tray or slot to hold the can.

Ten minutes pass. A willowy Asian man walks in my direction from the front of the bus and drapes the armrest of each seat on both sides of the aisle with white plastic bags. When all is done he marches back up front and exits the bus.

Outside the hollers continue.

"New York, Philadelphia, D.C.!" a woman yells.

"New York, Philadelphia, D.C.!" another follows.

"New York, Philadelphia, Hong Kong!" a third roars in fluent English. It is a male voice, and he sounds upset. "Shut the fuck up! It's fucking seven o'clock in the morning. People are trying to sleep, for Christ's sake! Money, money, money! It's always about the fucking money!"

Neck straight up, goose-like, I look outside. A gaunt Caucasian man with dirty blond hair storms the sidewalk with both arms folded behind his back.

"New York, Hong Kong, Philadelphia!" he thunders. "Who cares? I've been to them all. I've ridden your goddamn buses! They stink! They're slow!"

The women give the man disgusted looks and carry on their shouts.

The man barges up close and shoves his face at them. "Shut the fuck up!" he barks. "I'm going deaf!"

The noise finally dies down, and the sidewalk circus comes to a close. Thank goodness, there is peace at last.

Up ahead by the door a head pops up. My optimism plunges. It appears my worst fear has come true. A face I hoped not to see and did not want to see comes into view. It is the crazy man. He actually has the money to buy himself a ticket, and of all the buses, he has to choose the one that I am in. A New York trial lawyer books together with a crazy bagman. This is a nightmare come true. I am not ready for this type of company at this hour of the morning. Someone or something is trying to irritate me. In every corner of every street, in every section of town and in every hour a bagman is waiting. They say the devil takes different shapes and forms. This crazy man is probably the devil himself, but then again, there is no devil. There is only man and his insanity.

The crazy man, sweaty, his hands shaking, and his veins showing through, walks my way and stops two rows from where I am sitting. He mumbles gibberish to himself and hurls his bag onto a seat on his left. His lip curls in disgust and he blows out his cheeks as if holding back vomit. He curses at the world with the rage of a madman while bending over, removing his shoes, and tossing them onto the overhead baggage rack. His mouth runs as he goes through his bag. He scuffles and digs at its interior like it is the size of a football field. After finding what he wants, he hoists his arms in the air and tugs off his sweat-filled squalid shirt. Unbelievable! A hairy skunk of a crazy man stands half-naked and barefoot before my eyes. He is truly a modern-day Neanderthal. The man takes his seat and wears the wrinkly yellow shirt he removed from his bag. He has not showered in weeks. His body odors propel my way like meteors raining down on mother earth. No matter where I turn the fumes follow. He leaves me with no choice. I get up and move two rows back.

It is 7:30 a.m. A young Asian male, built like a football quarterback and wearing a Yankee jersey and chinos, makes his way into the bus and takes his seat across the aisle to my right. A row ahead in my direct view, a white male, mid-thirties, balding on top with a string of hair neatly combed across, also sits down. To his right on the opposite side of the aisle is a young couple. They look Korean. Maybe they are Japanese. Finally, there is an old Chinese woman and her husband, with a white baseball cap. The balding man slides over to let the old woman sit. Her aged husband takes a seat next to the crazy man.

One at a time, passengers gradually fill the bus. French, Indian, German, Spanish, Russian, and Cantonese quickly overlap. Before long the sounds become a drone. I would not have ever expected such an international turnout in a Chinatown bus. It is diversified enough to host a United Nation meeting. The night before, I envisioned myself being the only white guy on the bus. I pictured my big head sticking out like a sore thumb among the Asian crowd. I guess cheap tickets speak in universal tongues. There is no question the tickets are cheap. A taxi ride to Brooklyn costs more, yet I am going all the way to Washington.

It is eight o'clock. The sun is up. Outside, a white Lexus screeches to a stop. A black man in jogging shorts steps out from the passenger side and paces to the bus. The driver lets him in and closes the door. "Wait!" a passenger behind me shouts. I turn. Two Caucasian women race out of a yellow taxi and wave their tickets as they haul their luggage across the street. The driver lets them in and finishes his headcount. Now we are ready.

The driver takes his position. A loud rumble follows. Air spills from the overhead vent. It feels good. Outside, the rain fades. The sun warms my face. I slip on my headset, tune into a FM station, kick back, and dive into Tolstoy's *Anna Karenina*. It is light reading for the four-and-a-half-hour ride ahead. At least that is what I have been told. The trip could take longer. Maybe there will be a flat tire. Perhaps one of the old people will have a heart attack. There may even be a collision. Anything can happen on this bizarre bus.

Chapter 33

ON THE ROAD AGAIN

THE BUS HURRIES out of Chinatown and makes its way onto the interstate. It passes Exit 13. A short distance ahead on an advertising billboard is another thirteen. I turn left and look down. Inside a passing car on the back seat is a little boy. On the back of his T-shirt in red, balloon-size figures, is a thirteen. Retracing back to the young lady halfway in between, I pause. That is odd. How come I did not see it before? *Satan is laughing*, a scribbled message behind the old woman's headrest reads. Slowly but surely, a voice crops up. It is not coming from the radio, because it grows louder by the second. I remove my headset to trace the source of the gurgles. They are coming from the old lady. She yaps away in Chinese.

The young woman, sitting a seat across the aisle, attempts to calm the Chinese elder down. The cranky elder grumbles louder. Failing in her attempt, the young woman turns the other way and leans on her boyfriend's shoulder. I level my headset back on and increase the volume. The bus continues its course.

A few miles before Baltimore, the bus veers right and swerves off the interstate. The rest area comes into view. The driver slams on the brakes. The Chinese elder rockets from her upright position and plunges nose first into the rear of a seat ahead. That move finally shuts her up. The bus engine clatters cease, and the door swings open. Musty human odors thin out. I attempt to stand, but there is no sensation in my legs. I try again, holding on to the edge of the seat and pushing myself up. The blood circulates with prickly stings.

The elderly woman remains seated. Her legs must have given up on her, too. Mine did. Perhaps she is waiting for the crowds to clear out before she launches her attack on the hasty driver. It will be a good fight, but I am not sticking around to see the bout. Given all the boiling anger that has been building up inside her since the start of the trip, I am certain she will achieve a technical knockout. I can imagine her bony fist flying into the driver's face and crushing his jaw with a fatal blow. She probably would bite him if she could, but she has no teeth. Her husband, still wearing his baseball cap, stands up, turns, and signals her to follow. The elderly woman does not budge an inch.

I follow the crowd to the rest stop. It is muggy. The heat fizzles and the sweat sticks to me. I quicken my pace. A fast food restaurant closes in. The door slides open. It is cool inside. On the right is a long line for burgers and fries. On the left is the men's room. The food can wait, but the restroom cannot. I'd better make good use of the facility while it is clear. Who knows what lies inside the bus toilet stall?

I return to the bus parking spot, but where is the bus? I turn 180 degrees. There is no bus in sight. There is nothing but a few birds clinging to a barren tree that juts from the ground. The spidery roots swell the earth and crack the pavement. A few eighteen wheelers, pickup trucks, and motor homes sprinkle the nearly empty lot. I turn another 180 degrees. Wait, there it is, but it is further than I recall. Could it be the same bus? I walk. The vehicle comes into full view. The color is the same, and so is the logo. It has to be the same bus. I get on. Something feels different. Everything is the same, and yet something feels different. The passengers, they all look different. Where is the crazy man and the cranky old woman? In their seats are different faces. My backpack is gone. This cannot be the bus.

I look outside the bus window. There is no other bus in sight. I must have gone on the wrong side, but it is right. I have an impeccable sense of direction. Graduated Magna Cum Laude from Harvard Law; surely I can remember something as simple as the location of my bus. The driver must have left without taking a head count. The old woman probably pissed him off, and he decided to take off without her, too, but she is nowhere in sight, either. There is only one other explanation. Perhaps the old woman beat the dickens out of the driver and took the rest of the crew for a wild ride. The situation is absurd. Where the hell can they be? What am I supposed to do now?

"Stop!" I sprint forward before the door closes.

The bus takes off. I stand alone under the baby blue sky. Let's see what lies on the other side. I walk through the rest stop. I sigh in relief. There, next to a gas pump, is my bus. I get on and look around. Yes, indeed, this is the right one. The crazy man is here and so is the cranky old woman. She cringes in a ball and grasps her seat tightly. Her ear-splitting racket persists. The old man continues to ignore her. Lucky for him they are not seated next to each other. The balding white man to her left looks stunned. His string of hair is no longer in place. It dangles to the side. Why he will not cut it off, I cannot explain. I feel bad for him because he is trying so hard to keep from appearing bald. I also feel bad for him for sitting next to the old woman. There is nothing worse than having a pickled old woman griping away in broad daylight with a crowd watching. The horror, the discomfort, and the surrounding stares are never good.

People will look at anything that makes a noise. They will look at anything that moves. Whether out of curiosity, annoyance, disgust, or pure fascination, people will look. They look at each other, at themselves, and at those who disrupt the peace. I am one of them. I look because I am curious. I want to know what the hell is going on. I want to know why this old woman will not shut up.

How many words can come out of her mouth? I suppose no one wants to grow old. Time has an odd effect on people. It sours things and spoils even the most optimistic individual. Like a sweeping forest fire destroying the wildflowers, time will raze the green blush of youth and burn it to embers. Despite her earsplitting racket, I am glad to see the old woman. Her presence reassures me that I am not going crazy. There is no mistake that I am on the right bus.

The driver takes a second head count, and we are off. I put my headset back on. Willy Nelson sings: "On the road again."

Chapter 34

CITY OF TEMPTATION

A FEW HOURS LATER in D.C. the bus rolls to a stop. The crowd springs up to stretch. Almost everyone hastily fills the aisle and exits. The old woman is next. Her timid husband is a foot behind. I am not far from the two of them. Shades on, I step outside. My skin crawls in the warmth of the sun. I step aside and watch the crowds fight for their bags. The bus belly quickly empties. I would look for my luggage if I had any, but I have none. All I have is my backpack and two packs of Spearmint gum. Three have already been chewed. It has been a long ride.

I look around. No familiar face but those of strangers look past me. Their eyes gleam at the sight of their arriving guests. Where is my lead? Where is the woman I am supposed to meet? There are plenty of women around with long black hair. There are even more in blue jeans. It is D.C. Chinatown, after all, and most Asian women have long black hair. One by one I comb the crowd. Lanky, midget, waspish, buxom, pretty, and ugly, I question them all, including the locals who roam the street. I drill each woman and ask her if she is the mysterious person I am supposed to meet. Some understand English, and others shake their head. One even speeds away distrustfully.

The last passenger steps out. The hugs and kisses fade. The reloading begins. A fresh crew awaits the driver in his schedule-tight trip back up north to New York. The driver, leaning against the stair rail inches from where I sit, is getting his nicotine kick. Smoke billows from his mouth and nose. It must be his third cigarette since the unloading began.

"No more old woman," he says, showing a row of tar-filled teeth. "She coo-coo." He swirls a finger around his ear and walks off.

The bus wheels away. Fifteen minutes pass. Twenty minutes. There is still no one. The last of the passengers clears the street. This is ridiculous. Where the hell is she?

On the opposite side of the road, standing under a tree with leaves touching her head, is a young Asian woman. She is fairly tall. Add an inch or two to her heels, and she can match my height. Planos cover her eyes. The apple lips, yellow sarong, and black fishnets that wrap her defined thighs cry for attention. Her kaleidoscopic outfit matches the multicolored brick building that plasters the backdrop. She could very well be a local prostitute.

Maybe she is the woman that I have been expecting. She looks too classy to be a hooker. Whoever she is, it is refreshing to see someone like her. I admire a woman who is not afraid to express herself.

"Hi, I'm Victor," I say.

"Do I know you?" she asks, not threatened by my approach.

Disappointed, I return to my original post and sit on the corroded metal stair of a stranger's home. A few of the tenants come out of hiding and walk the block. Wait a minute. Why have I not thought of this before? The call history on my cell phone should have her number, whoever she is, that called the day before. I scroll the incoming call list and press the redial option. It rings once, twice, and three times. An automated voice recording finally responds: "This number has been disconnected. No further information is available at this time."

Another twenty minutes pass. She is not going to show up. It is a prank, and I fell for it. Sweaty from the heat, I look at the time. It is two o'clock. I must decide. The next bus leaves for New York in three hours. It is still not too late to turn around. There is no sense in spending a night in this city alone. There is nothing for me here. Why am I here in the first place? This is crazy. I am not ready for the return trip yet, though. It has been a long ride, and I need a rest. Besides, there is a chance she might be here. Perhaps she is behind one of those windows watching me and making sure I am alone. I'd better stay. I have to stay for at least a night. Exploring the city may not be a bad option, but with whom? I should have brought my college buddies' phone numbers. Several live and work in the area. We could have gone out and had a beer. It has been years since I've seen some of them, but if we meet, I will have to explain why I am here. They will laugh if I tell them the truth. Who in his right mind would go on a wild goose chase because of an anonymous phone call? After all, they knew what happened. They were there by my side eleven years before at Duke, carrying me through the bad time. That was then and this is now. First things first, I must eat. I am starving. I get up and weave up the street.

A block down the road to my left is a Chinese restaurant. It is a murky cave with hanging oval red lanterns. A few diners—men and women wearing black suits—converse quietly. In D.C., playground of the politically powerful and the intellectually gifted, one only has to keep an ear open to ease in on secret whispers about the world.

The waitress leads me to a window seat. I like the view. Outside, a woman tugs her poodle along. A man holding a parrot walks by, followed by a child licking ice cream. The waitress stands and waits. I turn the pages of the menu. "Beef tendon noodle soup," I say. "And a glass of water."

The waitress disappears into the kitchen. Shortly after, she returns with my food. "Careful, it's hot," she said. She steadily lowers the large bowl onto the table. Steam evaporates from the tangy broth. Mr. Chow, my work colleague and a fine litigation attorney, taught me the difference between traditional Chinese food and the

Westernized version. "Chicken liver is authentic," he said, "and sweet and sour chicken is not." To flavor things up, Mr. Chow taught me another secret. "Whether it's soups, salads, or stir-fried dishes, a few dashes of pepper or a few sprinkles of lemon juice will bring out the true flavors in foods." True to his words, Mr. Chow is right. As he always said, "Set the tongue in flame and the dragon will fly out."

The soup is filling. Recharged, I can think. I must decide. Stay or leave? Should I catch the next bus home or spend a night at the waterfront inn I had booked? I have to stay. It is too late to cancel the reservation. Why let a good room goes to waste? If nothing else, I can make good use of the scented soap and the clean towels. I need a cold shower anyway. I might even call room service and pamper myself with a nice massage and a strawberry sundae.

The waitress brings the bill. I hand her ten dollars and walk outside. "Taxi!" I holler.

An orange cab pulls to a stop. A head pops out.

"Where're you heading?" the driver asks in a thick Nigerian accent.

"Water Street," I say.

"Get in."

The driver speeds away.

Chapter 35

MARINA INN

I T IS A SHORT DRIVE to Marina Inn, a quiet place by the water southeast of the Tidal Basin facing the Washington Channel. Sailboats line the dock in the back beneath the boardwalk. I check in. The desk clerk hands me a key to my room.

My headache is growing. Damn the old woman. She did it. Her yapping still rings in my ears. Maybe it is not completely her fault. Maybe it is the summer heat and lack of sleep. I throw myself onto the bed. An hour later, I wake up. The headache is gone. I flip through the Shopping, Dining, and Entertainment Guide. Let's see. Top ten things to see and do—art and antiques, capital sights, dining, entertainment, sports, and nightlife. The phone rings.

"Midnight at Madam's Cavern at Dupont Circle," the Voice announces.

I jot down the address and glance past the sliding glass door. My eyes widen. I straighten my glasses to make sure. A woman has been looking at me the whole time. Legs spread, she sits on a white plastic chair by the poolside staring at me. Seemingly wearing nothing underneath under her summer skirt, she teases me with her legs. I am afraid to stir the see-through curtain. With a lift of the latch I can let her in, and we will no doubt have a good time. I know that is what she wants. "Come and get me," her actions suggest. "I am all yours if you only dare to let me in your cozy, pretentious and self-righteous world."

I want to have some fun. I can feel it, a feeling one has when alone in a hotel room. There is a bottle of champagne. There is a large oval mirror. There is classic mahogany furniture. There is a king-size bed, and there is me, sitting alone and half-naked on a chair inches away from the king-size bed. Outside, there is sweltering heat and the woman in the heat looking at me and adoring my body through the curtain. The only missing element in this picture is a link between our two worlds, a link to merge the warm and the cool, and to bring us together so that we can flare a kindling flame on the untouched bed. I want to ruffle up the nicely tucked sheet with her sugar brown body and smear her perfume all over the bed. I want to grab her by the neck and have a good time. Yes, I can see myself doing that. There is nothing a man like me would not do with a woman like her. I can easily let her in, but I cannot. Something inside me will not allow it.

Intolerable guilt sneaks up once more. It always does when I least expect it. I am afraid, not for me but for her. I, a predator with no conscience in the heat of the moment, know what I am capable of doing. I fear for her. I fear for the cleaning maid who has everything to lose and nothing to gain but fifteen minutes of good sex and fun. That is all I need, fifteen minutes. With fifteen minutes I will make her a happy woman. She will cry, scream, and even squeal. She will crawl the floor and climb the wall. I will make her feel what it is like to make love to a man like me, a man true to his art. Lovemaking is my gift. Like any God-given talent, if there is a God, I take it for granted. My father always told me that things that are easy to come by often get neglected. The same applies to the cleaning maid. If I am not careful, I will use and abuse her like the bathroom towels at my disposal.

The woman looks at me and waits for my response. I get up, put on my T-shirt, and walk away from the sliding glass door. For a moment, I had her fooled. I had her tempted and fooled. She thought I was about to let her in, but I did not. I disappear into the hotel corridor and return to the room with a bucket of ice. Outside the woman is gone. I run a cube down my forehead and let it melt. It feels numbingly cold. The heat in my body slowly dissipates. My sexual urge calms. I place my foot on the chair and stretch out next to the writing desk. The clock ticks. The time is eight o'clock. I have another four hours to kill. I turn on CNN. The reporter broadcasts more killings in Iraq. The world has changed since September

11. I know, because I was there that day, when the whole thing started. I was running the street like everyone else with the sky falling behind me. September 11 was a sad day, a day that marked the end of the world for most and nearly marked the end of my life. Lives were lost. Some people burned to death. Others were buried alive. All were killed within tons of melting steel and crumbling rubble when the two jets flew into the Twin Towers. The amount of suffering each individual endured before being consumed is beyond my imagination. I cannot begin to imagine the fear, the pain, and the last-minute scramble for survival before the world turned dark, but that was then and this is now. Now the clock is ticking.

Nine o'clock rolls around. I go to the back of the inn for a walk. Empty boats line the dock by the water edge. No one is around. I return to my room and check the time. An hour has passed. Two hours before midnight. Let's see what is showing on TV. The same news—the battle continues in Iraq. A car bomb explodes, machine guns fire, civilians run, and children cry. I switch the channel. An adult sex act is on. There is heavy breathing. The man mounts the woman. The woman moans. Animals, we are all animals without clothes. We are the grasshoppers, the crickets, the dogs, the kangaroos, and the lions. The only differences between us humans and those animals are our clothes, our reason, and our innovativeness. We can invent rockets and fly to the moon, but animals can only jump with their natural-born legs and fly with their wings to a height where gravity allows. We can inspire, and they can perspire. We can do it complex ways and in multiple positions, but they, the animals, only know one way. At least they are consistent and stick with what they know. And they do not have sex for pleasure or the wanting of pleasure but for reproduction. More importantly, they do not kill for politics, power, or religion, but only for survival.

Chapter 36

CATCHING AN ANGEL

I SHOWER, put on a black short-sleeved shirt and white kakis, buckle my belt, and walk outside. One thumb up, I hail a cab. "Dupont Circle," I order. Ten minutes pass. The cab stops at the corner of an intersection. I step out and the cab speeds off. Head up, I pace. A dozen blondes and brunettes rush in my direction. I walk faster. They catch up.

"Suck for a buck," one girl says.

Confused, I look around. All eyes are on me.

"Suck for a buck," the girl repeats.

"What?" I ask, befuddled by the sudden request.

"Suck for a buck." Her theatrical gesture brightens the faces of the surrounding crowd.

"No, I can't," I say, looking embarrassed and wondering why she is flaunting her chest at me. Things clear up.

Gummy bears dangle from her shirt like Christmas tree light bulbs. There are twenty, thirty, maybe forty colorful gummy bears with strings.

"Am I not pretty enough for you?" the girl asks.

"No, it's not that."

"Suck! Suck! Suck!" the crowd cheers.

The exhibitionism must be part of a Georgetown sorority rush, but it is summertime, and some of the girls look older than college age. A few even have wedding rings.

A petite one, perhaps five-feet-three with fair skin and puppy brown eyes, and wearing a micromini, grabs me by the arm. "I'm Ginger," she says.

"Nice to meet you, Ginger, but I have to go."

"Come on, it's only a dollar." Ginger presses herself onto me and refuses to let go.

"It looks like I'm not going to get out of here without further resistance, am I?" I remove my wallet and look inside. There are fives and twenties. "Anyone have change?" I ask.

The girls search their purses. "I have two dollars," one finally confirms.

"Okay, two should be sufficient." I hand the girl my money and attempt to break free from Ginger.

"Oh, no, you don't," she says, still holding on to me. "You have to suck now that you paid."

I look around. People in the street stop walking and look my way. The girls circle me with their cameras ready. "No pictures!" I insist. They reluctantly lower their cameras. I bend down and snatch a piece of gummy bear from the girl's shirt. The crowd claps and cheers.

"Two more," a tall blonde urges. "A dollar for each piece. You paid for three."

"One is enough, thank you." I feel nauseated. God knows where the piece I swallowed has been.

"Where are you heading?" Ginger asks.

"Nowhere." I look at my watch. It is 11:20. I have forty more minutes to kill.

"Are you alone?"

"I'm visiting a friend in town."

"Where's your friend?"

"He's at home packing. He has an early flight tomorrow to Boston."

"Why don't you come with us?" Ginger offers, hanging on to me like I am her boyfriend.

"No, I can't." Again, I try to break free.

"Come on," Ginger pleads. She throws me a puppy look and tugs me along with a hand around my waist. The others mosey farther down the street. Ginger and I trail behind. Several blocks down I stop.

"What's wrong?" Ginger asks.

"I better get going."

"Why so soon?"

"Because—"

"What is it? It's Saturday night. Don't you like my company?"

"I do. You're a knockout. In fact, I'm the luckiest man in D.C. tonight to be surrounded by all these gorgeous women, especially you."

"Why do you have to leave so soon then?"

"I just remembered that I have something to do."

"Are you sure you don't want to come with me?"

"You're a sweetheart. I would love to, but I really have to run. It's important."

"Okay." Ginger reluctantly let go. She pecks me on the cheek and walks away.

It is ten minutes until midnight. In a retracted corner of an alley a brawny man in black suit guards a door to Madam's Cavern. He looks serious, serious enough to toss a 180-pound man around without breaking a sweat. "ID," he croaks, both hands folded behind his back.

I show him my driver's license. He throws me an icy glance and clears the way. Behind the door a dark cave lies. Red lighting illuminates a small stage at the center of the floor. On the stage a pert striptease wiggles, leers, and swirls on the metal pole. As she slides upside down, a scantily dressed melon-breasted waitress approaches me.

"Good evening," the waitress says. "This way, please."

We stroll pass the stripper toward a square table three tables away from the main stage. I take my seat. Back facing the wall and perpendicular to the stage, I glance at three newcomers entering the joint. No one I expected.

"Would you like a minute?" the waitress asks.

"Yes."

The waitress takes off and walks toward the rear of the room. A smaller section juts from the corner on my immediate right. Straight ahead a middle-aged man sits alone drinking his beer. Forty-five degrees to my left are two men, each accompanied by a stripper. They talk, and the women nod and pretend to be engaged in the conversation. I hear the women's fake laughs, forced upon them not by the men's jokes but by their sheer obligation to entertain their guest. My gaze returns to the food and wine menus next to the overflowing ashtray. The prices are outrageous, but I have to buy something. Nachos with chicken sounds good.

I signal with my hand. "Waitress?"

She walks over. "Are you ready?"

"Yes. I would like number fifteen."

"What would you like to drink?"

"A Coke would be fine," I say. I must stay sharp. Alcohol will blur the mind, and I am not going to take that chance.

The waitress disappears to the back. Shortly after, she returns with my drink. I remove the paper wrapping from a straw and dip the straw into the ice-filled glass. Another dancer struts on stage. She is young, sculpted, and vivacious. She prowls the stage like a black panther, bows, and steps away from the spotlight. Another dancer makes her way up. Ten minutes pass. There is still no one recognizable in sight. A few regulars scatter here and there. They smoke, drink, and talk to the girls. One appears to be enjoying the view.

At last, my food arrives. The waitress hands me the plate of nachos. It is a large plate mixed with melted cheese, onion cubes, sliced chicken, chopped tomatoes, and shredded lettuce. I munch on the nachos. They are not great, but at least they are filling. Too bad there is no salsa. A little dash of hot sauce to spice things up would make the nachos taste much better.

One by one the girls walk by and introduce themselves. None are the one I am looking for. I shake their hands and let them go. There has to be a sign, any sign. Another dancer walks on stage. A cone-shaped light shines on her dark straight long hair, light skin, and perfectly slim body. My heart beats faster. She is beautiful. The music starts. She dances to the gothic beat of *Enigma*. I have never seen anyone move like her before. Sultry and sensuous, she turns and teases. She is a sheet metal woman doing a fan dance. As she does her moves she looks at me.

I gasp. "Incredible."

Another half hour passes. There is still no one and no sign. I order another Coke and continue to munch on the nachos. "Be sure to chew slowly," I tell myself. "There is still time to kill." I look around. The eyes in the cavern, they know me. They know I am not here for the women or the food. The food sucks. It lacks flavor and freshness. It is stale like the raw air that I breathe, air filled with souls of lonely men and lost women, and air choked with cigarette smoke and alcohol fumes. I feel like I am in some kind of weird dream, but I am reluctant to wake up just yet. I am mesmerized by the surroundings. I sit in a

Zen-like state taking tiny sips of Coke. My heart slows to a rhythmic beat. I am calm but alert.

"Hi, there," a voice crops up from behind.

I stop chewing and look up. It is the exotic dancer. She is more beautiful off stage than on. Her creamy skin stands pale against her jet-black hair, red lips, and two-piece leather outfit. Unlike the others, she looks innocent and sweeter than maple syrup. She must be new in the field. My gut says so. The gut never lies, deceives, or betrays. The mind can analyze, reason, and persuade, but the gut only reacts, the ultimate form of objectivity.

"I'm Angel," she says. "May I join you?"

"Please." I slide over.

Angel squeezes next to me on the booth and bends over. Her head tilted and her chin up, she unzips her shiny knee-length boots to expose her skin. "It's hot in this thing," she says, stripping free of the black boots and returning to her upright position. Her legs are soft and light. A black elastic band wraps around the upper part of her left thigh. Strapped inside the band are crumpled dollar bills, mostly ones and fives, bills tucked into her garter by the hungry hands of men. "Do you have a name, handsome?" she asks.

"Don't we all?"

"What is it, then?"

"Does it matter?"

"Very well, I'll give you one. Let's see. What shall I call you?" Angel places her head on my shoulder. "I know. I'll call you Achilles."

"Do you do this often?"

"Do what often?"

"Pretend like you're drunk to seduce men."

"Why would I do such a thing?"

"I don't know. Why don't you tell me?" I run my finger up her tender neckline to her chin and gently press her lip to show the white of her teeth.

"I like your glasses," she says, studying my Gucci frames. Light feathering breath expels from her mouth. Her eyes, I know those eyes. "Are they real?" she asks.

"Yes."

"Where did you get them?"

"Manhattan."

"I love the Big Apple. It has everything. I take the Chinatown bus there once a month. The Red Dragon Express costs forty-five bucks for a round trip. You can't go cheaper than that."

"Where do you go shopping in Manhattan?"

"Guess."

"Let's see. A girl like you would probably go to Fifth Avenue."

"Nope. Try again."

"SoHo?"

"Wrong."

"Times Square?"

"What's in Times Square except the wild teenage girls that clutter the sidewalk of Broadway outside the MTV studio screaming their lungs off? There are no shops there."

"What do you mean there are no shops there? There are tons of shops there."

"I meant shops with stuff that I want."

"If not Times Square, then where?"

"Boy, you're more persistent than a woman."

"It comes with the profession."

"Very well, if you must know, you have to promise me not to laugh."

"Okay."

"Chinatown."

"Why Chinatown? It's crazier there than Times Square. Have you seen the Saturday afternoon crowd? Add to that the traffic noises, the dust, the heat, and the smell."

"I go there for the fake handbags. I don't care about the noise."

"Why not buy the real thing? Fifth Avenue has plenty of stores that sell handbags."

"Do I look like the type of girl with hundreds of dollars to spend on a handbag? I'm fine with my forty-dollar Fendi, thank you. In Chinatown, I can get fifty for the price of a real one, one for every occasion. Anyway, enough about my handbags, tell me about yourself."

"What do you need to know?"

"Where were you born and raised? You're not a Yankee; I can tell."

"What's that supposed to mean?"

"Your voice, it has a tiny southern drawl."

"I grew up in a small town in North Carolina."

"How long have you been in the big city?"

"A few years."

"What do you do there, if you don't mind my asking."

I do mind, but I will tell her anyway. I will tell her because the whole thing between the two of us is a play, an act, and a mind game. I want to amuse her and keep her company. If I play my game right, my prize will be the disclosure of untwisted fact. "I make sure that justice gets served," I say.

"You're a lawyer, aren't you?"

"Maybe."

"Are you a cop?"

"Perhaps."

"I know. You're an FBI agent."

I laugh. I am in no hurry to satisfy her inquiry. Let her guess. I want to see what she will say next. The night is still young.

"Is that why you're here in D.C.?" Angel asks. "You're here on an important mission, aren't you?"

"How can you tell?"

"You handle yourself well."

"How do I handle myself?"

"I don't know. You're such a gentleman. I feel like I can trust you. You're not flaky like the others. I know sincerity when I see it. It's an unspoken fact that shows in the eyes, the body gestures, and the tone of voice."

"Looks can be deceiving. Don't trust everything you see."

"I know, but I'll do myself a disservice if I fail to disclose one grain of truth tonight."

"The truth is nobody can be trusted. Humans are natural-born liars. How far or how deep we're willing to stretch the truth depends on the circumstances."

The waitress walks by. "Another Coke?" she asks.

"Yes," I say. I turn to Angel. "Would you like something to drink?"

Angel points to the wine list. It is her job to order the most expensive drink on the list and get her client to pay for it. Joints like this make money that way, but she is considerate enough to wait and let me make the offer. She is also thoughtful enough to order a moderately priced white wine. The waitress takes the order and leaves. Another loner walks into the cavern.

"Tell me, what is a nice girl like you doing in Madam's Cavern?"

"It's only a part-time job. I'm actually a student at Georgetown."

"Really?"

"Yes, really. Why are you looking at me like that? I'm telling you the truth."

"I believe you."

"No, you don't. You can't fool me."

"What are you studying at Georgetown?"

"Literature. I'm finishing up my master's. I'm also writing a book."

The waitress comes out with the drinks. She steadily lowers them on the table and returns to the back.

"What kind of book?"

"It's an autobiography," Angel says.

"Aren't you a bit young to be writing an autobiography?"

"I have an interesting life," Angel says. "Do you see this?" She leans closer and points to a fading mark above her left brow.

"It looks like you got whacked by one of those horny bastards."

"Shut up! I got this in New Orleans. Some idiot threw a cabbage at me. It was the size of a freaking basketball."

"That's funny."

"No, it's not. It hurt like hell."

"I'm sure it did. What were you doing in the heart of tornado alley?"

Angel sips her wine and places her hand on my lap. "Partying like everyone else. Me and the girls, when we were students at UNC Chapel Hill, we drove there every year."

The city brings back memories of Mardi Gras, wine, women, and sleepless nights. Angel was also there, four times. She bares her experience in the former French quarter and unfolds stories of the mudslide, the bars, the partying, and the sex. She has done it all. She was the wild child I once was, after my separation from Siren. I did it to kill the pain. Angel did it for the game.

"How far are you with your book?" I ask.

"Nine pages."

"That's progress."

"You don't believe me, do you?"

"I believe you."

"No, you don't. Go ahead and ask me anything. I dare you."

"What can I possibly ask you? My grasp of literary knowledge is limited."

"You're a smart guy. You read. I'm sure you can come up with a question."

"How long have you been doing it?"

"Doing what? Writing?"

"Doing what you're doing now."

Angel glances over her shoulder. "Three weeks. What does it have to do with my book?"

"Nothing."

"Okay, if you must know, things got fairly bad. I needed the money. I was behind on my rent."

I look away and think about Siren. She, too, was hard pressed for money. My gaze returns to Angel. "How does it feel having to bare it all and have total strangers touching you night after night?"

"It was hard at first," Angel says. "But like everything else in life, you get used to it. I learned to separate myself from society's expectations. What's right and wrong became irrelevant. Have you ever freed your mind and pretended that the body you occupy is only a container holding flesh and blood?"

"No," I lied.

"You ought to try it sometime. It's liberating. I remember doing it for the first time. I bared my chest to a crowd at Mardi Gras. They loved it, and I loved it."

"Tell me how you first got into this business. How did they prepare you?"

"They start you out slow. They make you rehearse in front of a large mirror in the dressing room by yourself, then they put you on stage with the other girls. I was shy at first, but I got over it. It's only a job, I told myself. You've got to make a living somehow." Angel looks at ease, not at all bothered by the fact that she is disclosing her personal life to a total stranger she barely knows.

"What about those close to you? How do they feel?"

Angel looks left, again the look of suspicion, and returns her attention to me.

"Mom and Dad don't know. They're too busy trotting the globe. The last I heard of them, they were in a car somewhere in North Vietnam passing through rice fields dotted with colorful cemetery vaults."

"I have never been to Vietnam."

"Me neither, but from what I heard, it's an exotic country." Angel talks about the trucks, pedestrians, bikes, motorcycles, and oxcarts that fought the dirt road and the hot sun.

"Where were your parents heading?"

"They were on their way back to their hotel in Hanoi from their trip to Landing Dragon Bay. It was quite an excursion. Mom said it took them over four hours by car and two ferry crossings."

"Landing Dragon Bay sounds familiar. I read about it somewhere. Isn't that where they have the oddly shaped limestone islets that stick out of the water?"

"Yes, over 3,000 of them. Legend says that these islets were formed by the swish of a dragon's tail."

"How often do you get to see your parents?"

"Once every three months. Mom got me this from The Khan el-Khalili, one of the oldest markets in Egypt and in the world." Angel lifts her arm to display a charming bracelet on her wrist, a gold-plated antique.

"Does your boyfriend ever get jealous or worry about your safety?"

Angel looks away. The girly charm disappears and a somber Angel takes over. "We're no longer together."

I reach out and touch Angel's hand. It feels cold. Something tells me she still loves him. It is within human nature to love what is lost.

"Do you ever get lonely?" Angel asks.

The question strikes a nerve. Yes, I get lonely. I get lonely all the time. I get lonely even when I am not alone, but she does not need to hear another sob story, not from me. I am sure she has heard plenty already, as part of her job. Her job is to listen and sympathize. She must be sick of sympathizing.

"No, Valerie keeps me company," I say.

"Is she your girlfriend?"

"No."

"Is she your wife?"

I show her my fingers. "Do you see a ring?"

"She must be your lover."

"Val is my secretary."

"Secretary, huh? There must be some hanky panky going on between you two. There's nothing better than having hot office sex on the copy machine on a late Friday afternoon."

"That's with the cleaning lady."

"For real?"

"I'm joking. Don't get me wrong. I'm not the type of man I used to be. There's nothing between Val and me or the cleaning lady."

"You mentioned her name. There must be something going on. The subconscious never lies."

"Val has a little crush on me, but it's only an innocent crush. You know, the type a younger girl has on an older man, but it still feels good to be wanted."

"I think it's sweet that she finds you attractive, but are you sure the whole thing is only an innocent crush?"

"I swear on my dead parrot's grave. Comfort is vital in a healthy work environment, and I would hate to let Val go because I feel uncomfortable being around her."

"Define discomfort."

"Discomfort can be an encroachment of my personal space by someone I find repugnant or have too much attraction for. A man cannot be productive when another part of his body other than the brain is doing the thinking. My rule of thumb is never play around in a workplace, even if there is great potential for a long-term relationship."

"What are you afraid of?"

"Things can get nasty. People might gossip in the office. It might affect my work. I don't want any of that to happen between Val and me."

"What's wrong with having a little fun now and then? You're a man. She's a woman. You're single, and she's single. You both have needs. What's the point of living if you can't shack up?"

"It would be a shame to lose someone like Val."

"Is she that special? You can always find a new secretary."

"Val is irreplaceable. She does flirt occasionally, but she knows when to draw the line. My objective is to serve my client to the best of my ability and in the most ethical manner. Her goal is to help me achieve my objective in the utmost professional and efficient manner. Efficiency can only be achieved through a disciplined, healthy working relationship."

"Who said that working relationships aren't healthy when sex is involved? Sex spices things up. I refuse to believe there's no touching or groping between you two."

"Val knows better. She may be young, but she shows tremendous restraint. I don't know how she does it. I wish I had that type of self-control when I was her age. Bad as I was back then, I'm getting better now. I realize that there are consequences."

"I still don't get it. What does Val have to offer that other girls don't? You're young, handsome, and smart. Why do you think so highly of a secretary? Any girl can type."

"Val entertains me with her liveliness. There's something about her that lights up the room. Her energy radiates and brightens everything she touches. She affects everyone around her and makes work less dull. Considering the long hours I spend in my office, I need someone like her. A little smile here and a little pat on the back there really make a difference. Her presence makes the coffee taste better. It gives me the extra boost in the morning to start the day."

"I have to give it to you. Certain people project great aura. This line of business has taught me a lot about people. Some can walk into a room and immediately drain all the energy. Others fill you with joy."

"Val is not only free spirited, but also dependable. She gets things done right the first time, and fast. It helps with my hectic workload."

"How long has she been working for you?"

"Slightly over a year. It's a year and ten days, to be exact. She graduated from Columbia University and decided to take time off from school before going to law school."

"That's smart. Hey, at least she has a good mentor who refuses to take advantage of a sweet little pumpkin like her. Who wouldn't want to work for a nice, good-looking attorney like you?"

"I'm not nice, and how do you know I'm an attorney?"

"Come on. Who are you kidding? I knew you were an attorney the moment I set eyes on you. Do you think I'm just some dumb bimbo with big boobs? Don't be fooled by this beautiful body. There's a brain in here."

"I'm not questioning your intelligence."

"What made you go into that God-awful profession anyway?"

"It's a long story but here's a short version. Hector, who is a friend of my father and an acclaimed immigration lawyer, gave a lecture at Duke in the summer of 1993. Hector mentioned to my father that he needed a hand. My father suggested that Hector take me under his wing for a summer, because I had nothing else lined up. I was pretty messed up back then, and he didn't want me moping around the house doing nothing. Thinking that a trip to the bay area would clear things up, I took the offer."

"I have a question. I heard that immigrants are devious and dishonest. Is that true?"

"Yes and no. I had the same question, initially, when I heard rumors of how some of them manipulated their way into this country through lies, bribery, and other means of personal, professional, and political influences. That's why I joined Hector's firm. I wanted to see first-hand how things really operate and see whether any of what I heard was true."

"Were you surprised by what you learned?"

"Surprised, no. Disillusioned, yes. Immigration law has its appeal, but it's also disheartening to see how things actually work. It's an intricate political process with high stakes for both parties. It's the U.S. government versus potential shadow enemies as well as law-abiding foreign citizens traveling and entering our semi-well-protected borders. The influxes of foreigners, good and bad, into this country through legal and illegal means amazes me. They arrive in commercial planes, human cargoes, fishing boats, and even by foot. Everyone wants a piece of the freedom Lady Liberty offers. Most are good and some are bad, but all want in and few want out."

I look at the clock. It is two a.m. I slip Angel a twenty-dollar bill. She takes the money, folds it in half, tucks it inside her bra, and hugs me. It is a genuine hug, and it feels nice. It has been a while since I truly felt something for a woman, and of all the places and people, it has to be a stripper inside a nightclub.

"You better go to the other men," I say. "I have just enough to cover the food and drink."

We look around. A few men are scattered here and there, the same faces and the same crowd.

"What other men?" Angel asks.

"It's a slow night, isn't it?"

"Yes." Angel leans her head on my shoulder, not caring whether anyone is looking. "You're nice. I like talking to you."

I sit back, hold Angel tight, and wait for the woman that I am supposed to meet. Another fifteen minutes pass. Angel gets up and disappears to the back. The waitress clears the unfinished nachos and brings out the check. I flip it over. In the back, barely visible, is a message: "Trust not your eyes but your heart, my love. It is time. Be at the rooftop of the Sky Club in half an hour." The name, it seems familiar; it is the name of the club across the street from where I had left Ginger. I remember looking up and seeing the sign.

Once more I walk the night streets. Straight ahead a short line forms by the door edge of the Sky Club. I take my place, show my driver's license, and walk past the bouncer. Floor by floor, I work my way up. Trance, DJ-spun house, hip-hop; they have it all. I squeeze pass a swirling mass of salsa dancers in a smoky room and head for the rooftop bar, an interesting outdoor setting with soft lighting and fake palm trees. Laid back jazz musicians play their gigs. A sedated crowd sits in wicker chairs drinking, talking, listening, and relaxing to the music. I walk up to the bartender and order a cold beer. Wedged in at the balustrade, I peruse the bird's eye view of the city's nocturnal skyline. It blinks with lights, tiny lights like tiny stars. I wait. I wait some more. I continue to wait. No one shows up, no messenger, no message, nothing. Just before I am about to give up, the dark hair girl shows. It is Angel, and her high-pitched voice is no longer the same. In its place is the voice I heard over the phone, Siren's voice.

Part VI

A TIME TO HEAL

Manhattan 2003

Chapter 37

STONECIPHER DEBACLE

L ove is war. It is war against God, if there is a God; war against the world; war against the heart; and war against those you think you love. From a seed of love, a child is born, a tree grows, a thought inspires, a disease infects, a desire possesses, and chaos unfolds. Like a black vulture lurking in a crimson sky or a headless dancer making men cry, or like a crescent moon unmasking in fright and a lost soul devouring its own light, love is war. In the shadow of a steady falling rain where lights dim, Theotokos cries, doves die, and footsteps crawl, love expels its dragon breath. Its radiance outlasts the millennium's rain. Its moon-like shine holds an angel's glow. Its luminance shimmers the tributary's flow. With love the earth swells with joys and tears. Love swallows a woman's fears. With love, stars glow like a newborn's eyes, and its energy travels a trillion miles. With love the cedar cradles and sways its *branches. With love the meteors spray in needle-like strains, and their lights pierce the heaven's veins. With love the rain dances with a cobra's finesse, and its movement puts a man's trouble to rest. With love the wind howls, the thunder roars, the snake hisses, and the goddess squirms. Love is war. It is war against God, if there is a God, war against the world, and war against the self. At the peak of love, one tastes a sweet flavor of heaven, if there is a heaven. The reality that follows is the sour aftertaste of hell, if there is a hell.*

Eleven years ago, a day following our trip from Minnesota, Siren disappeared. Everything in her room was as it was when I last saw her. A withered rose lay slanted in a marble vase on her window ledge. A coffee mug lay empty on her writing desk. Chucky, her favorite teddy bear, remained half covered underneath a white sheet on her bed. To the right of her writing desk, pushed tightly against the wall, was a shelf heavy with books. Above the shelf on the wall, evenly spaced between two oval mirrors, hung a replica of *Le Violiniste Bleu* in an antique gold-toned frame. Marc Chagall, the Russian-born French painter, had always been Siren's favorite. His style of suffused poetic fantasy in a dreamlike world reflected her inner state of mind, a mind where the door revolved around the awake and the asleep, the real and the surreal, and the practical and the ideal. Siren was the type who would be perfectly content living in a small rented room in a foreign hostel of some quaint town where artists and intellectuals dwelled. When night rolled around, she would go to some bohemian spot where people of all ages gather and dance the night away. Such was the personality and personification reflected in her choice of art. Such were the structures of her life.

Months following Siren's odd disappearance, I waited. Behind a closed door I waited. I circled my room and waited. I sat crouched on my bed with a pillow on my stomach and waited. I waited for the familiar holler and the sound of her footstep. "It's only temporary," I told myself. "It won't be long. She'll find her way home. There's no doubt that she'll return."

Seconds ticked away. Minutes went by. Hours strayed into days. Days turned into weeks. The door remained untapped, the phone stayed silent, and the mailbox remained empty. No letter or messenger informed me that she was all right; neither was there any clue of her whereabouts. There was nothing but me, a pathetic and lonely fool sitting alone in a room waiting for a woman I thought I knew.

Slowly and surely, anticipatory thoughts and apprehensions took their toll. They disrupted normality and poisoned my thought with suicidal ideation. Life turned into a living hell on earth with no end. Agitation, restlessness, and paranoia filled my waking hours. Nerve wrenched and mind crazed, I turned for help, but the reality continued to unfold. No antidepressants, psychotropic drugs, alcohol or meditation could soothe the pain, because a part of me refused to let her go. I clung to the possibility of hope and staggered drunkenly in a permeable world of transitory obsession. I convinced myself that things could be the same as they once were.

Sometimes late at night, I felt Siren's feathery breath teasing my skin. I felt her hand running along my back. I felt her warm body sliding next to me. When I rolled over for a kiss, though, she scampered out of sight. I grasped empty air. The sound of piano playing ceased. Silence once more instilled the air. The hushed autumn leaves sailed buoyantly to the ground. They fell in the hundreds and in the thousands. They fell until they touched the wet earth, home of the worms, the maggots, and the apple trees. I then had an epiphany. The mind once more tricked me. It was only a dream, a byproduct of a wishful thinking for the existence of an invisible being, so I attempted to calm the secret yearning of an arrogant mind, a mind that refused to let go and a mind that continued to hold onto an illusion of what could have been.

Loneliness and melancholy returned. They cloaked the night with phantom wolves. These monsters resurrected in new shapes and dangerous forms that sucked me back into a terrifying vortex of time. Reason warped, and thought twisted the dark alleys, besieged passageways, and choked city tagged along the leafless winter of fear, the fear of being alone and having no one to understand me. Cold, trapped, and gut wrenched, I once more felt the familiar stirring not of love, but the loss of love. The storm of human emotions loomed from all sides. In the dead of the night I sat and cried. It was not within my nature to cry. I was a man, and a man was not supposed to cry. I cried anyway. I let it all out like the torrential rain. I cried because I knew that something was terribly and irrationally wrong. I cried because she had to leave me so young.

Since the first day we meet, I had always loved Siren. I loved the way she walked, the way she talked, the way she laughed, and the way she arched her neck back when she laughed. I loved her scintillating jokes and the scent of her perfume and how it excited me. She was the light within my rimmed building and the ominous footstep in my empty street. She was the black-headed nightingale whose lightning-fast wing beats lightened my day. Most important of all, she was my little star who stood like an opulent church in the sky. She was all that and more. For the longest time, I wanted to tell her how important she was to me, but something inside me held me back. Maybe I was afraid. Maybe I was embarrassed. Perhaps I was too arrogant. I thought I had time. Whatever the reasons, I waited until it was too late.

My attempts to erase Siren from my mind only brought back more memories. The more I tried to forget, the more I remembered. In the journey into the mind, I remembered. What else could I do but remember? Memories were all I had. Memories of our time together clinched onto me like a deadly parasite sucking the life out of its host. I felt her imminent presence watching me and haunting my waking hours. Somehow, I knew she was not happy. Her troubled ungodly presence sought out to reach me. She wanted to tell me something, but I did not know what. There was nothing that I could do but close my eyes. In the dark cavity of my room, I held onto my bed and pretended what I experienced was only a bad dream. I reflected on the many nights we had dozed off together. I thought about the mornings we had awakened to see the red ring of the sun. There were the Saturday morning cartoons, the pinball games in the corner store, and the water balloon fights. On cool autumn evenings, we snuggled up and watched the leaves fall from the comfort of Keith's reclining chair. It felt nice to have her on top of me. Her scent, her touch, her breath, and the first nostalgic notes of Beethoven's "Moonlight Sonata" all felt nice.

Music was her life, art was her soul, and astronomy was her spirit. She once said we each have a responsibility on this earth. Whether it was to catch lightning bugs or watch the stars, we must carry out our role. If we could only meet again once, I would try to make things right. All I needed was a second chance, but all I had were hopes and dreams, empty hopes and hopeless dreams. No whisper, no touch, and no sensation. There was just the unending numbness and the pouring rain.

Over the years, I questioned what I used to know about Siren or Katerina, as she would say. How much did I really know about the person I naively professed to be "the one" and had allowed myself to fall in love with?

"You're in grave danger," Siren warned when we first made love. "Run away while you can. I'm not good for you."

What did she mean she was not good for me? What kind of woman would say such a thing to her man in such a moment of intimacy? More importantly, what kind of people was she dealing with that caused her to say such a thing? What did they have on her that she feared so much? Was her warning made out of sympathy or was she compelled to say it because of guilt for manipulating someone she had grown to love? What about those people we met or those she had spoken about? Who were they? Was Nikolai really her uncle or Nadia her great aunt? The childhood stories, were they all fabrications and lies, too? Who was the thick-bearded man I saw on the Chinatown bus? There were more like him in the library, in the restaurant, in the bar, on the road, and even in distant towns. There were as many of them as the raindrops from the sky. Were they all part of a vast shadowy network run by Jack, the mob-connected lover who preceded me in Siren's life, or other notorious and conspiratorial forces that would do anything to hide the truth? The truth lies in the mind of one person, Siren.

When Siren disappeared, the men and women I came to know through her also were gone. Nikolai, Joe, Buddy, Nadia, the priest, the hermit, and Mr. and Mrs. Schmidt, were all gone. All phones were disconnected, and all houses and apartments emptied out. No trace was left, as if they never existed and I had been living in an eerie wonderland, a wonderland where my love for Siren had taken me. These people, whoever they were and however in-

significant roles they played, all contributed to my understanding of life and love.

A graduate of UNC Chapel Hill saw Siren the night of
her disappearance eleven years ago. It was an August
night of full moon. The UNC graduate was standing outside "Tender Night," a Franklin Street bar, when a black
convertible pulled into sight. A slim and handsomely built
man wearing a sport coat stepped out of the car and
walked her way. Something about the man caught the
graduate's attention, the distinct mark on the man's left
cheek that resembled a knife scar, and the intense look in
his eyes. He seemed as if he was about to plot something
big. Curious, the graduate followed him upstairs. The
man stopped and glanced at an old signboard above the
door before entering the smoke-filled room.

Inside the bar the man took a seat in a dimly lit area. He
remained to himself, smoking his cigarette, listening to
the soothing sound of saxophone, and hawking the
women in the room. A young woman in a black dress
approached him. He whispered into her ear, and she followed him outside to his car. The graduate trailed their
car up and down the winding streets. They drove past an
old quarter of town, crossed a railroad track, and sped out
of Chapel Hill. The convertible finally stopped, and the
two made their way through the woods surrounding Fall
Lake. The graduate, within an observable distance, saw
three men in black joining the two at the edge of the lake.
One shined a flashlight on the young woman's face, and
the other two grabbed her from behind. She kicked and

screamed to fend off the men's attack. They dragged her into the water. Frightened by what she saw, the graduate took off and called the police.

The cops arrived too late. A life flight helicopter scanned the vicinity with no luck. A team of scuba divers was dispatched the following day. They spent the afternoon dragging the water. Before the dive had to be called off because of the encroaching night, a duffel bag was spotted at the bottom of the lake next to a tree trunk. Inside the bag was a torn black satin dress with several strands of hair on it. DNA tests showed the hairs matched the one Siren had given me. She plucked one out of her head the night after we made love for the first time. "You'll need this someday," she said. I thought she was joking but I kept it anyway. I placed it in a matchbox and kept it safe.

No one knew what really happened to Siren. I could only guess. The night before her odd disappearance, I dreamt a knife-bearing assailant climbed through her bedroom window and attacked her. She fought back. She spat blood, and then she was dead, hanging lifeless from a wooden clothing rod with a piece of rope coiled around her neck. I had often dreaded this terrifying moment. I knew that something bad was about to happen, but did not know when. The intricate lines of her palm were filled with the violent intricacy of the universe. Every river and stream on its maze-like surface spooked with hidden dangers. Like meshing strings, the lines first had a look of certainty and predictability, but the harder I looked, the more chaotic they became. At the end, the strings led to one point and one destiny, Siren's fate.

I named a tree after Siren. She stood between two other oaks. Her barren trunk bulged from the earth and twirled high into the sky like the figure of a farmer's wife sowing seed. On windy nights, she swayed gently with a light sweeping motion, taunting me with her playful hairline branches. Perhaps she was trying to tell me something. Perhaps she was attempting to shake free of the great evil that had consumed her life.

Siren once sang me a French song about a drowned sailor whose soul is being plucked from the water by a seagull. The bird flies toward the sky in its attempt to deliver the sailor's soul, but the bird could not fly high enough. "That explains the awful sound the seagull makes," Siren said. "It is the sailor's trapped soul that desires to be free."

For most of my life, I had convinced myself that nothing greater than man existed. Siren's absence stirred in me a series of ageless questions we had often discussed. "When we die, will we be remembered for the good we have done? Why are we placed on this earth? Is there a God out there?" I found myself questioning the very belief she had so strongly held. "If there is a God and if he causes all to exist, then where does he comes from, and what right does he have to take her away?"

"There is no God," I told myself in my darkest hours. "Until the silence of impending death punctures the last palpitation of my heart, my belief shall stand firm. When that time comes, I will divorce myself from this physical world. With a final measure of vengeance I will turn my head away from possible salvation if there is a God, and let my eyes slowly sink below the horizon without any fear of violent reprisal from life itself. No crowing rooster or ringing black telephone will be able to wake me up again."

Someone once told me that to be content with life a man must first kill the thing he loves. Unfortunately, my mind will not allow me to do such a thing. My love for Siren is eternal. It shall remain unshakable, even in the final second of my life.

My time with Siren far exceeded my expectations. It took off like a racecar moving down the quiet road of life. While zooming along, it hit a bump and spun out of control. When I thought I knew it all and had it all, things failed, the world collapsed, and a familiar face disappeared. I scrambled for logic and explanation, but there were none. All that was left were the names implanted deep in the rich soil of my subconscious mind. Through these names were intricately netted memories, lots of unexplored memories of Princess Bay, Huguenot, Great Kills, and Old Town.

Love, fragile as it may seem, is an enigma. The nature of its innocence and the brutal strength of its tenacity quicken the heart of even the most arrogant being, the human being. Like the rise and fall of the Roman Empire, one moment we are at the pinnacle of love, and the next we are at the abyss of loss. The hurdling arrows of love plummet deep inside our shell, lacerate our flesh, tear our veins, and splinter our reason. In the moment of grief, we are wiped out of existence by the almighty arrows of love. Like a hollowed corpse beneath the soil, we remain lifeless with no marker to remind the world that once we were happy in this lonely world.

It is within nature's will to return love to the earth just as it was found, naked and organic. Someday, love will once more crawl through my arteries and veins like water siphoning up the roots of a plant. Someday I will taste love again like the lush field of grass tasting the radiant sunlight. Only then will I be free of anger, worry, and loneliness. That someday is now. My Siren has returned, not as Siren, but as Angel. In a world of an interminable dream, my Angel opens new doors and carries me under her wings.

MEMORIAM

W E ALL CRIED. We cried out of joy, sadness, or fear. We cried the moment we first laid eyes in this world because we knew that life was going to be tough. Inside our mother's womb, we could only imagine what the world holds, but when reality struck us with the first breath of air and the first sight of light, we fought in fear and desperation. We wailed as loud as we could in hope that someone would hear us, listen to us, and understand our concern. No one listened and no one understood, though, so we struggled our way back inside our mother's womb, a place of flesh and blood free from the pain of humanity, a place we called home. But it was too late. Out of the darkness of our transitional phase, a pair of hands stripped us free from the cave that had housed us since the beginning of time. Cord tied and body soaked, we were brought into this world not by choice but by fate. Thus, we adapted and dwelled in our new world, a place filled with untold promises of love and a place of chaos that arose from the loss of love.

ACKNOWLEDGMENTS

I T TOOK FOURTEEN YEARS, from the conception of a thought to its final draft, to give birth to this book. Along this long, bumpy journey, the number of U-turns I made, the pieces of napkins I used, and the types of people I met are as many as the tributaries branching from the Mississippi River. Completing a novel of this magnitude would not have been possible without the encouragement, critiques, and support of countless individuals. They are students, artists, singers, theater performers, ministers, lawyers, politicians, doctors, and writers, to name a few. A short list of these individuals includes Alison, George and Friends in Staten Island, New York; Angela in Atlanta, Georgia; Allegra in Philadelphia, Pennsylvania; Mary and Family in Durham, North Carolina; Christina and AP English Class in

Atlanta, Georgia; Kimberly in San Diego, California; and Nancy in New York, New York. Further, I want to thank my internationally diverse and exceptionally talented group of editors, including Ruth Lexton from England; Alexis Korman from Canada; and Patricia Lespinasse, Marisa Parham, and Bobbie Christmas from the United States for their critical analysis and technical editing during the early or final phase of writing this novel. Finally, I must thank my family for its extraordinary patience.

I have read, referred to, and or used resources including books, magazines, newspapers, and Websites while writing this novel. Some places simply serve as reference sources for information about historical or geographical facts and events, while others provide insightful ideas about scientific theories, philosophies, and religion. Some of these resources include *The Meaning of Life* and *More Reflections on the Meaning of Life* (compiled by David Friend and the editors of *LIFE* Magazine); *The New International Webster's Pocket Quotation Dictionary of the English Language*; *The Chronicle* (Duke University's newspaper); *Biography*; *People*; *Time*; *The Holy Bible* (Nelson's revised standard version); and *Russia, Ukraine & Belarus* (Lonely Planet Publications travel guidebook). In the final chapter of this novel, the referral to the French song about a seagull that attempts to deliver the soul of a drowned sailor to heaven is from a quote by Melvin Van Peeble (Actor & Director) printed in *Life Special: Searching for the Soul*. Other lyrics or songs in the book, unless specifically mentioned otherwise, are my original works.